SOUTHERN
INTRIGUE
at *the* LOCAL
GREEK DELI

CHARMAINE F. LECLAIR

Library of Congress Control Number: 2020919798
ISBN: 978-1-945587-63-4
First Edition

Fiction
1. South Carolina—fiction
2. Greek Food—fiction
3. Italian Opera Buffa—fiction
4. Local Officials—fiction

Book Design: Dancing Moon Press
Cover Design: Dancing Moon Press

Dancing Moon Press
Bend, Oregon USA
dancingmoonpress.com

DANCING
MOON
PRESS

DEDICATION

In loving memory of Will Moredock

Acknowledgements

When I moved to South Carolina in September of 2002, I felt as if I had entered a foreign country. Being from Oregon, Charleston, presented more of a cultural shock to my system than Mexico did when I lived there for eight months in 1986. After a number of years observing the bizarre juxtaposition of various cultures in this Deep South landscape, and scratching my head about why some South Carolinians still seemed to be fighting the Civil War, I happened upon a history book on the topic entitled *First Blood: The Story of Fort Sumter* by William Swanberg. I never would have opened this book before moving to the South, but after finishing it in one weekend, Swanberg became my favorite author. I have included many of his unique and hilarious turns of phrases in my first venture into writing.

My friend, Lee Pringle, Founder of the Charleston Gospel Choir and the all-black symphony orchestra, Colour of Music Festival, invited the brother of the opera star Leontyne Price, George B. Price, to Charleston to give a talk in 2018. It was at this delightful presentation that I heard and then used direct quotes about Mr. Price's life growing up as the famous diva's sibling.

Ron Menchaca and Glenn Smith penned an excellent article about the Sofa Super Store fire of 2007 for the Post and Courier which I used as a reference. Although, just for the record, I was working at my husband's Greek restaurant across the street during that fire, and it did, in fact, take twenty minutes for the first fire engine to arrive, in contrast to the timeline that they reported.

While writing *Southern Intrigue at the Local Greek Deli*, I imagined it being narrated with a particular Southern drawl, the distinctive accent of two South Carolina public radio personalities who promote Southern culture, Walter Edgar and Tut Underwood. It would be a thrill to have either one of these men narrate this novel for an audio book.

My husband's niece's late husband, Will Moredock, is the author of *Living in Fear: Race, Politics and the Republican Party in South Carolina* as well as *Banana Republic Revisited: 75 Years of Madness, Mayhem and Minigolf in Myrtle Beach* and was a regular political columnist for the City Paper of Charleston for many years. I couldn't wait to ask Will to edit this book, knowing how much he would get a kick out of this satire on Southern culture. Unfortunately, he succumbed to a sudden, unexpected and rare illness before I had the chance to show him the manuscript. But, in spirit, Will's political humor guided me along to the final draft.

Finally, thank you to my mom who read the entire manuscript aloud to my dad, and who then cheered me on to the final product. Thank you!

—Charmaine Leclair

CHAPTER 1

Unbeknownst to the fine-spun people of Port City, South Carolina, a modest town chartered in the 17th Century, which politely hugged the Atlantic Ocean with Southern hospitality, the unpresuming storage shed that was lodged in the parking lot of the Local Greek Deli was an ideal haven for long-kept secrets. The edifice was erected innocently enough alongside the fence of the Old City Jail which had been condemned long ago since the year 1880 when it was no longer deemed fit to house even the most offensive prisoners.

No one is sure if the shed, with its matching architecture, originally resided on the well-manicured property of the Old City Jail that also accommodated a cemetery dating back to the Revolutionary War. It did appear to be intentionally erected to compliment the beauty of the sprawling live oak trees with the dangling puffs of Spanish moss. In particular, it seemed to have been built to partner with an underground storm shelter approximately one hundred feet to its left. But at some point, when a gaggle of unscrupulous Local City Councilmen from years past met behind closed doors, some underhanded gerrymandering was executed, resulting in the county line being moved an extra twenty yards to the South, making several voters' opinions moot, and one small structure added to the list of assets for the Local Greek Deli.

The building was composed of stone mountain granite, the same material that comprised the dilapidated prison which had once housed infamous robbers, murderers, and pirates of the high seas, some of whom died in captivity, and others who escaped and were never apprehended again. The final group of boarders to occupy its cells, before it was declared unsuitable for use, consisted of a hundred Union prisoners of war transferred from Georgia during the concluding months of the Confederacy. The jail was now celebrating its one hundredth anniversary as the host destination site for the Port City of South Carolina's most popular and lucrative tourist attraction: The Walking Ghost Tour. The Old City Jail was haunted; to be sure, the residents who lived in its quaint historic borough would attest. The Locals would come lean on the railings of their high piazzas, while the well-rehearsed tour guides led groups of gawkers through meandering paths on the cobblestone streets.

On each side, the homes were painted various complementary pastel shades of the rainbow. Some of the residents had worked out a small commission, and would entertain the people enjoying The Walking Ghost Tour from their verandas with their personal yarns of spirit sightings and frightening sounds that surely originated from the disturbed souls of the disembodied inmates. A nickname for the Old City Jail was The Keeper of Secrets, because of the many unexplained mysteries that surrounded the peculiar three-story stone building, shaped like a vertical hair curler, whose cells were still fitted with huge chains bolted to the walls that rattled ominously during evening thunderstorms.

The one secret that the jail has held most tightly to its bosom is the disappearance of Mayor Moe Smiley, Sr., who was elected in perpetuum for 68 years straight, and had been in the running for another term, aiming for a satisfying 70-year stretch, when he fell upon misfortune. The last anyone saw of Mayor Smiley was him inspecting the grounds of the Old City Jail during the aftermath of Hurricane Hugo to see the extent of injury the massive storm had inflicted upon it. People are still speculating if it could be his spirit that regularly clatters the chains at night in hopes of rectifying his plight.

In spite of all the tall tales created by the neighbors, most of the Locals were a tad skeptical of the lore affiliated with the Old City Jail. Not even the historic district's most prominent resident, the gusty, 80-year-old, supercilious Local City Councilman was satisfactorily persuaded of their veracity. He himself believed solely in the gullibility of the Yankee tourists, and appreciated the steady revenue that they ushered into the small port city of South Carolina. Otherwise, he merely scoffed at the superstition associated with the Old City Jail as pure rubbish.

However, today, this particular Monday in June when the no-see-ums were biting and the humidity made the heat insufferable, the Local City Councilman found himself drawn to the idea that the Old City Jail could provide him the service of harboring a secret. He was almost ashamed of himself for believing, even for a moment, that an old deteriorating building could possess the power to conceal his misdeeds. But today, he felt desperate, and he succumbed to the intrigue of the legends. He had run out of options, out of time, and out of friends. He needed to find a furtive place for his secret to remain unexposed. A place where, even if revealed, everyone would surely attribute the disreputable activity to the Ghosts of the Old City Jail. It would never be connected to him.

As he navigated out of his driveway in his double cab Dodge Ram 2500 4x4 truck with leather seats and an elaborate thousand dollar painting of the Confederate flag adorning the back window, he ventured out to the prison with such urgency that the large yellow flag with a coiled snake proclaiming "Don't

Tread on Me" flapped wildly in protest from the pole next to the shotgun rearview mirror. The Local City Councilman was unaccustomed to feeling on pins and needles. He had never felt moisture on the palms of his hands or sensed the thumping of his heart in his chest. He had spent his days in unflappable self-assurance, with all hints of self-doubt mastered and well in hand. He was undecided on how to take the reins of this unfamiliar onset of jitters resulting from his current mare's nest. While ruminating at a red light, he stretched across the cab, pushing aside papers in the glove compartment, and determined to take a swig from his flask to placate his fluster.

Suddenly, he shook his skeptical head in disbelief. He was amazed at his good fortune. As he was approaching the curb by the Old City Jail, he spotted the unassuming shed on the opposite side of the fence that belonged to the Local Greek Deli, a pillar of the vicinage in Port City, South Carolina, for over thirty years. By nature, the Southern statesman did not let himself buy into the idea of luck. Like most political leaders from South Carolina, he was born into wealth, in an atmosphere of heirlooms, from a long lineage filled with servants, slaves, pride of heritage, and reverence for family honor and State rights. Luck had nothing to do with whether things went his way or not. He believed that if you were born into the right family, then as long as you did your part to honor your clan and the Palmetto state, then everything would naturally go your way. But, today, he wondered if it was his worthier lineage or mere happenstance.

The Local City Councilman, who was proud to serve and mingle on the friendliest of terms with the populace of the moderate, urbane Port City of South Carolina, was known as "The Honorable Counselor Dr. States Rights Gist V, Esquire." Among his peers, he was simply called "The Fifth," for he was the namesake, the great-great grandson of the famous Confederate General of distinguished eminence, the one and only, General States Rights Gist, who died a noble death in one of the first battles of the War Between The States in the year 1860. The Fifth refused even now, upwards of one hundred and sixty years later, to dishonor his great-great granddaddy by ever committing blasphemy against his family by calling this war, The American Civil War.

A born incendiary and skilled propagandist, The Fifth was the proprietor of the Local Right Wing Rag and weekly podcast, *The Herald*, where by virtue of the First Amendment, he was free to print and spew his verbal campaign against anything that resembled human decency. Using his Herald as a torch, he played on his readers' touchy sense of Southern honor as well as their feelings of racial superiority. His readers would risk their lives to help save a puppy drowning in the harbor one day, yet turn around and reminisce about the good ole days when lynching wasn't considered murder, during the very next. And with the sincerity that only a true zealot possesses, he convinced them all that they were right, even when this premise implied that everyone else was wrong. Whether in print or in person, The Fifth proclaimed his political views with such monomaniacal persistence that even most of his colleagues thought of him as a hot-headed crackpot.

But The Fifth was not without a particular political shrewdness, much in demand among politicians of all complexions and countries. He knew to demonstrate the wisdom, however vulgar, to know which side of the bread is buttered, even when the matter at hand, in all its phases and bearings, had a strict outlook for the well-being of only a few insignificant citizens, for this wisdom could be construed in his favor when times were turbulent, so as to keep the public from noticing his unsavory activities.

Such was the case ten years past, when his sails were trimmed to catch the then predominant political breeze, and he proceeded to the dominion of the Mayor and succeeded in convincing him to refurbish all the downtown sidewalks to have wheelchair access at the street corners. The Fifth paid for the opening ceremony of the first completed concrete indentation on the South corner of the Four Corners of Law in the center of hustle and bustle, posing for selfies with properly bribed wheelchair-bound residents. He posted the photos on *The Herald's* website, to document his uncharacteristic generous move, and to enlist the spirit of the otherwise refined people of the Port City of South Carolina to continue electing him onto the Local City Council. Year after year, the constituents of Port City were cajoled and finagled into tolerating this full-time agitator, The Fifth, rather than follow their natural inclinations to put a muzzle on him.

So The Fifth considered luck as a childish proposition, except on this particular Monday summer evening in June, when he saw that the door to the mountain stone granite storage shed in the parking lot of the Local Greek Deli had been left open. The wooden door was swinging lazily in the breeze, tapping lightly against the frame in random rhythmic intervals. A small green gecko scurried across the frame with lightning speed and concealed itself in a small hole in the hinge. A huge cockroach, with wings to fly, locally known as the "Palmetto bug," ran for cover as it dove into a crack in the floorboards. The Fifth, upon seeing this, quickly changed strategy and rather than park next to the underground storm shelter adjacent to the Old City Jail, he decided to drive to the other side of the fence. He peered through the Dodge Ram windshield and surveyed the Local Greek Deli's parking lot. He eyed the back door to the restaurant to see if any employees were venturing in or out of the business, and seeing no one, he was satisfied that the coast was clear. He could stash his secret in the shed, blame it on the immigrant dishwasher of the Local Greek Deli if anyone were to accuse him of malfeasance, and that would be the end of it.

With his familiar haughty sense of impunity restored, he pulled up his latest model Dodge truck next to the open door of the granite storage shed of the Local Greek Deli. The Fifth began unloading his burden of humiliation from the covered truck bed, first by sliding over to one side, and then placing onto the ground, the leather case which cradled his prized Anschutz 1781 rifle in velvet-covered memory foam that he accepted in lieu of cash payment at one of his clandestine gambling games, and which he used to the demise of several wild hogs in the Francis Marion National Forest. Then he spread his arms wide and clutched onto each side of the bottom of the large, black canvas bag that was big enough to conceal a young adolescent boy. And being that it was fragile, he had to use caution as he stepped to the right, slid it out of the truck, and set it gently onto the ground, so as not to damage the object of his culpability.

The Fifth's shrinking 80-year-old frame was only half as tall as his enormous guilt-laden black canvas bag, so he had to grab the narrow top of the receptacle and drag it a few inches at a time until he finally maneuvered it into the storage shed, disposing of it along the back wall, behind the top-loading freezer that was filled to the brim with Greek-style boneless, skinless chicken. Only a few inches of the thick fabric remained exposed, but it was positioned in the darkest corner of the shed. Someone with a keen eye would be the only one to notice it.

The Fifth thought he heard footsteps, so he made haste out of the shed and brushed himself off, trying to appear unruffled. His heart was pounding, but he maintained an attitude of nonchalance as he looked around the back of the shed to see what was there. He walked to the other side and peered around the corner. He stood on tiptoes to look over the bed of his truck in order to see the street side of the Deli, searching amongst the sago palms trees that lined the restaurant for the source of the noise. No one.

A sharp whack of the shed's door on the frame made him jump with a start. Convinced that the footsteps were a figment of his currently sensitized imagination, he opened the door to the Dodge Ram's driver's seat, where his yellow lab, Old Heller, named in honor of the Heller Decision of the U.S. Supreme Court to strike down the Washington D.C. ban on handguns, was waiting patiently. As pets tend to do, Old Heller had carefully positioned himself directly on top of the broad peak lapels of The Fifth's navy blue, pinstriped, linen, double-breasted jacket with gold-buttoned cuffs, releasing copious amounts of fur onto the tailor-made blazer that he wore daily, regardless of the informality of the event at hand. In his heightened state of awareness and breathlessness from exertion, the sight of Old Heller sitting there with his tongue hanging out, smiling and panting, so expectant and loyal, eagerly thumping his tail, brought a lump to his throat in an unexpected rush of emotion.

The Fifth had purchased his canine friend from one of his devout fire-eating Herald readers from the upstate of South Carolina in an effort to awaken desires in his beloved beaux-to-be, Miss Pettigu, and convince her to take his hand in marriage, something he had hungered for his whole life. But to his dismay, when the day arrived where The Fifth had worked up his courage to ask for her hand, his fantasy was not in alignment with what came before him. He had arrived in eager anticipation with Old Heller at the Local Dog Park where Miss Pettigu could be found each morning with her eleven-year-old pug, Watson. As he galvanized his inner chivalry, he reminisced about their first conversation at the park.

"Mornin', Miss. Seems as if you could have chosen any beautiful breed of dog alive, but you chose the one with the ugliest face known to man."

Her silence. So genteel. The mark of a truly cultured aristocrat.

"I voted against the proposition to use this city block for a dog park five times in a row. What nonsense to waste perfectly good public space for a bunch of mutts to lay their excrement," the Fifth continued in his effort to stir her advertence.

And straightaway, she recognized who he was. "You must

be that pompous windbag City Councilor, States Rights Gist," she retorted.

He gasped in bedazzlement. Definitely, this was a highbrow gentlewoman, knowledgeable about local politics and current affairs. She indeed deserved to be his wife, thought The Fifth with sparkles in his eyes.

But when he drew near her that fateful day, he was aghast to see her arm in arm with another man. And a Yankee at that. She was so beautiful, so fair. Her elegant, poised sixty-something demeanor was always cultured and somehow very calming. The Fifth knew he would never be able to find another woman as wonderful in the few remaining years of his life. He had fantasized that they would be wed on December 5th, the late Senator Strom Thurmond's birthday, but to no avail.

The photo of Miss Pettigu that he had taken of her without her knowledge on his I-phone, remained attached to the Dodge Ram dashboard, fading more and more each day in the rays of the South Carolina sun, just like his hopes were fading each day for their wedding ceremony as he watched her stroll away with that scoundrel Yankee on her right and that mutt pug, Watson, on her left.

Swallowing his sentiments, he noted the humidity and the perspiration that he had worked up, then he thought better of putting on his double-breasted jacket, and instead tugged it out from underneath his faithful four-legged companion and tossed it to the back cab. He sat behind the steering wheel for a few moments, composing himself and refocusing his attention to the details at hand. He was feeling satisfied that his secret was now stored securely within the parameters of the Old City Jail.

As he took another sip from his flask, he felt an unanticipated wave of remorse for what he had done. The weight of abusing his position of power and taking advantage of others less fortunate than him suddenly tightened his chest. He wondered if the burden of the secret was worth it. Why was it that he never felt satisfied with what he received in life? Why would he, someone whose entire span of time on earth was nothing less than halcyon, still feel so empty? Why was life such a cycle of disillusionment? He stroked Old Heller absentmindedly as he considered these inquiries. But being that no exegesis came to mind, his rare moment of reflection quickly passed. He shifted the gear into drive, breathed a heavy sigh of relief, and revved the engine of his American-made truck. For the first time in his 80 years on the planet, The Fifth considered the idea of divine Providence.

◉

Old Heller's smile disappeared from his faithful face as he let out a long-sustained growl and positioned himself to attack.

"What's that all about, ole boy?" The Fifth asked. He knew his dog assumed this stance whenever the owner of the Local Greek Deli was nearby. Ever since the councilor made the mistaken presumption that it was permissible to feed Old Heller an entire skewer of marinated lamb kebab, and was chased down the street, the Fifth's best friend was no friend at all of the restaurateur.

As he looked to see who the recipient of the dog's warning was, Old Heller broke into a fit of loud barking. He saw the same thing. The last of a swiftly moving trace of a person and a silhouette of his prized Anschutz 1781 rifle disappearing into the mountain stone granite storage shed. Precisely at that moment, the owner of the Local Greek Deli pulled into the parking lot, putting The Fifth into a quandary.

He realized that he could not pursue the shadowy character into the storage shed for risk of disclosing his secret, which left him with no other alternative but to drive away, and leave behind his prized firearm to the mysterious crafty thief. He strained every nerve to appear composed as he taxied his latest model Dodge Ram into the main road. His assuredness about his newfound luck dwindled as he sped away, with Old Heller barking furiously in tow.

The pint-sized sixty-year-old restaurant owner always adorned with his black wool Greek fisherman's cap and neatly groomed salt and pepper handlebar moustache that was waxed at the ends to dangerous keenness, as happened on occasion, did not notice that the Deli's kitchen had run out of garlic over the weekend. In the world of Greek restaurants, an event such as this befalling the kitchen required swift action. He had immediately reacted and was returning from the Local Piggly Wiggly supermarket with fifty bulbs of garlic, enough to subsist on through Thursday when the Sparta Import Foods truck would deliver the next weekly supply of 200 bulbs.

Now, he did, in fact, see The Fifth's large American-made truck with the yellow tread-fearing snake flapping in the wind out of the corner of his eye. But Monday night was the regular night to see The Fifth at the Local Greek Deli, and he was deep in thought from his morning's events, so it did not cross his mind that The Fifth's normal arrival time for their weekly Monday night poker game at the Local Greek Deli was not for another two hours.

The long-ago immigrated Greek Persian restaurant owner, Mr. Olive, as he was called by the people of Port City, South Carolina, for they were much too polite to admit that they could not pronounce his name, was known on his passport as Mr. Nazoon Susa Kalamatamidas III. His reputation centered around his sententious elevations of his interminable oratory that revealed unsurpassed pride of his heritage. Even The Fifth had to yield to Mr. Olive's hubris when it came to bloviating about family roots and his victorious motherland. Nazoon proudly claimed that he could trace his family lineage all the way back to 324 B.C. during Alexander the Great's invasion of the Persian empire's capital city of Susa. Though The Fifth never dared let on that he was dubious about Nazoon's claims to glory, he'd patiently listen to the oft repeated narrative.

Nazoon explained that the original spawn of his tribe was from the union of one of the Greek conqueror Alexander's close associates, named Zues, with a captured Persian noblewoman named Zarbanu. Members of Nazoon's family tree branched off of the Greek Orthodox Church into Islam sometime during the Eighth century AD. Nazoon declared that one of the statues in the British National Museum was of a relative of his, a traditional Muslim arbiter, a mufti, from the time that the famous Greek Parthenon served as a mosque during the Fifteenth century.

Mr. Olive could recite the entire two thousand, three hundred and forty-four years of the maternal branch of his ancestry, not only by name, but also by the delectable Mediterranean dishes these women were known for serving. He was currently working on publishing a book filled with the mouthwatering recipes of each dish of his matriarchs. By the time Mr. Olive finished pontificating about his heritage and describing the ambrosial flavors of the fresh garlic, oregano, and tomatoes of his favorite grandmother's souvlakis, falafels, and hummus drizzled in lemon juice from lemon trees that stemmed from cuttings dating back to Alexander's gardens, then showing off his sapphire blue and white, evil eye kolomboi worry beads with the image of Cleopatra engraved on them, which were always passing through the fingers of his left hand, after all of that, even the most courteous Southern debutante could not stifle their yawn. But stifle it they did, for if anyone insinuated that Mr. Olive's Greek family was not worthy of their rapt attention, they risked a headlong boot out the door of the Local Greek Deli with a kebab tomato thrown in their direction.

Mr. Olive drove past the mountain stone granite storage shed and parked his meticulously maintained Mini Cooper Clubman in his reserved parking space that was next to the gerrymandered fence that separated his business from the Old City Jail. But he did not notice that the storage shed door was unlocked and left open, and swinging gently on its hinge. He was normally an observant fellow, but his mind was preoccupied with his appearance in small claims court that morning.

He was replaying the events of the proceedings as he carried a plastic grocery bag filled with garlic, and his ever-present kolomboi worry beads in one hand. In his other hand was his trusty myrtle wood hand-carved walking stick custom made to fit his hand that was slightly deformed from birth. A former disgruntled employee, a certain Señora Concepción from México, a middle-aged, never-married woman who was very pretty for her age, but wore just a little bit too much powder on her face, took on a waitress shift at the Local Greek Deli to supplement her small business selling antique piano sheet music. Despite her better judgement, Señora Conche, as she was commonly called, had become just a touch enamored with the long-time widower Mr. Olive. She knew they had little in common, and he showed no signs of fancying her in that sort of way, but she optimistically would spend hours preparing him offerings of homemade pan dulce, chicken chipotle, beef mole stew, and other delectable dishes she learned from her Abuela in México as a young lassie.

After a few months of these overtures passed by unnoticed, Señora Conche discovered that her food was being consumed by the cooks and other waiters, and sometimes even the regular customers. Mr. Olive never sampled even a single morsel of her pan dulce or chicken chipotle specialty. To add insult to injury, she overheard him grumbling one day, "That damned Gordita keeps bringing me unappetizing grub she learned to cook from the wrong side of the river. I wouldn't feed this wetback slop to The Fifth's scroungy mutt, Old Heller!"

In response, bolstered by a wounded sting of vengeance in her heart, Señora Conche tossed a Mythos beer bottle on the floor, faked a fall on the liquid, feigned a broken ankle, and then proceeded to file a workman's compensation claim against the Local Greek Deli. And with the fury of a scorned unrequited lover, Señora Conche set out to take Mr. Olive to the cleaners.

Now, Mr. Olive was a litigious man himself, so he was not unfamiliar with these modes of action. He was also a landlord who had taken unfortunate tenants to court many times. Even using The Fifth as his legal counsel if it seemed a winning proposition to do so. He knew how to file the paperwork for a lawsuit in his sleep, whether for something as small as not sending payment via certified mail, or as big as not giving him thirty-one-days-notice to vacate. Nazoon prided himself on how he could work the system to squeeze every last penny from the lowlife that rented his properties, or anyone else he deemed to be blameworthy.

But this former employee, this particular conniving waitress, La Señora Conche, possessed that mysterious woman's intuition for spotting weaknesses in the men who jilted them and won the case against Mr. Olive sitting pretty. The Local Judge, who had overseen one too many court appearances of the owner of the Local Greek Deli, declared, "Mr. Kalamatamidas, it looks as if your greedy misguided notion of justice has been handed back at you. Here's a little taste of your own medicine. I expect payment to be made in person every month on my own desk. Is that clear?"

Not once had Nazoon lost a case, and it made him purple to have someone out-shyst him in the courtroom. Fuming over his losses, Mr. Olive walked right past the lurking gecko and Palmetto bug without even a second glance. He propped open the back door of the restaurant with his walking stick, entered the back door of the Local Greek Deli that led to the kitchen, and lay the fifty bulbs of garlic on top of the stainless steel prep station table. He nodded to Ernest the chef, grumbled at Malik, the prep cook, and offered a gruff hello to Mahogany, one of the musicians he had hired last year to play live music for his patrons twice a week on Mondays and Saturdays.

Mr. Olive was so annoyed with the court order to pay off that deceitful, opportunistic, underhanded Señora Conche that he didn't even notice that the usual din of the Monday Night Regulars at the Local Greek Deli was silent. Not a peep was coming from the dining area, but he proceeded to the bakery in the back of the restaurant to sit in his swivel chair, put his head in his hands, and calculated the effects of this newly acquired debt. He figured he'd need to sell at least twelve more pieces of Spanakopita a week to indemnify the Local Judge's wrath.

He lifted his head, and hanging next to the 80-quart Hobart mixer that produced weekly portions of hummus and cake batter was a photograph of Little Zora, his three-year-old granddaughter, the apple of his eye. The photo was taken only a few moments before the accident. Zoraki, who never knew her grandmother, for she had long since passed on to heaven, called her grandfather, Mr. Olive, "Ya-Ya," which delighted him to no end.

The accident was no one's fault, but everyone who was there took the blame. Especially Mr. Olive, for the last words little precious Zoraki uttered before she slipped and fell in the swimming pool were, "Ya-Ya, Watch me! Watch me!" Then, right before everyone's eyes, Ya-Ya, the mother, the father, and extended family watched in horror as Zoraki disappeared under the water, weighted down because her little foot somehow had become tangled into the leash of the family dog who was being choked by the descent of the granddaughter.

The father dove in immediately, released her foot from the leash, and rescued her in five minutes. But in that portentous five-minute period, Zora lost her ability to move, see, speak, or swallow. She now lay motionless, 24/7, in a medical retreat for children called Home of the Angels. Mr. Olive went there every morning without fail and rocked his silent beautiful Zoraki in his lap for two hours before heading to the Local Greek Deli.

As he wiped a tear from his cheek, Mr. Olive had a fleeting moment of doubt that this court loss was for a reason other than just an ill-prepared case. When the Judge was chastising him, it was disconcerting to him, he had to admit. It had never occurred to Nazoon that getting justice for himself could result in injustice for someone else. Maybe it hadn't been necessary to submit all of those legal petitions.

He shook his head to brush off the preposterous and uncomfortable notion. That didn't make any sense, he reasoned with himself. He picked up the newspaper and tried to distract himself from the unfamiliar feelings of regret. As he perused the daily courier, he did not hear the loud slamming of a door with a bang. Therefore, he did not get up to investigate, and so he remained unaware that his custom myrtle wood hand-carved walking stick that had been propping open the back door of the Local Greek Deli was now nowhere to be seen.

CHAPTER 2

The commotion in the dish room carried on as usual. The haphazard collision of plates against bowls continued at an ear-piercing volume as they were shoved into the dishwashing machine followed by the thin metal door slamming shut with a resolute thud. The rhythmic whirling swishes of the water engine provided a near constant backdrop hum to the kitchen in the adjoining room of the Local Greek Deli. The good-natured, twenty-eight-year-old, Seattle-born violist, Mahogany, unaffected by Mr. Olive's dour mood upon his return with the fifty bulbs of garlic, had greeted him warmly as he walked by.

"Hello, Mr. Olive. It's good to see you." Hearing no response, Mahogany shrugged and raised his eyebrow at Ernest, who was banging spatulas on the grill preparing a pork souvlaki.

Ernest just shook his head, and noted from experience, "Oh boy, it's going to be a fun night."

Mahogany's shoulder length blonde hair was clean yet perpetually unkempt atop his slender frame. He regularly sported a tie-dyed rainbow t-shirt, pants purchased at Goodwill and Birkenstocks for shoes, which gave him the appearance of someone ten years younger. His soft spoken, gentle, and humble demeanor veiled the estimable intellect and enviable talent he possessed as a musician and scholar. No one is sure where Mahogany acquired his musical inclination. Unlike Mr. Olive or The Fifth, he was not steeped in generations of family lore. An only child, his common law parents were married unofficially at an International Indian yoga retreat ashram officiated by a holy man of undocumented credentials.

They were farmers of organic hemp in rural Washington, who enjoyed telling little Mahogany as a child how he was conceived during a camping trip at the Oregon Country Fair. A place where clothes and deodorant are optional and pot smoking and African drumming are mandatory. They didn't even give him a legal name until he was five years old. They let him choose his own name on his fifth birthday. His mother was not certain how her son came upon the word "Mahogany," or if he even understood that it was a tree, but she gave her blessings for his choice of moniker and immediately went to the Seattle city courthouse to sign the legal documents to make it official.

Mahogany only knew sparse details about his family tree. From what he could ascertain, his paternal great-great grandfather left France during the French Revolution as a pacifist. He made it to Canada, travelled West until he hit British Columbia, married a Cree Indian woman while veering south, and settled in Yakima, Washington. There, he and his new bride created a wheat ranch with several sheep, and sold their wool to Pendleton Woolen Mills just over a hundred miles away in Oregon.

With this scant knowledge of his ancestral roots, and having no one like Alexander the Great as a family friend from 324 B.C., nor having a fallen Confederate General's spirit haunting multiple generations with pride and prejudice, Mahogany thought it reasonable to credit his prodigious musical abilities to someone who was not even of blood relation. He gratefully acknowledged the source of his talents to be the grace of his meditation teacher, Swami Lafalottananda of Southern India, the spiritual guru of the uncredentialed holy man who unofficially married his common law parents.

Ever since Mahogany was a young child, he assumed that he was a reincarnation of the Hindu Goddess Saraswati, the bestower of Knowledge and Music. His neon yellow fiberglass viola case was adorned with several images of the beautiful four-armed deity with her veena and swan. His apartment had statues of Saraswati in all types: wooden, bronze, and ceramic, sitting on every flat surface in every room, adorned with candles, fresh flowers, and incense. He recited long-winded, complicated sanskrit mantras dedicated to Her powers, and glorifying Her attributes every single morning, and before every single music practice session.

Upon meeting Mahogany, few would suspect that he held a faculty professorship at the Local Community College of Port City, South Carolina. Ever since he began playing dinner music for the patrons of the Local Greek Deli, most of them, The Fifth included, merely presumed that he was a homeless hippie that had wandered in off the street. Ernest, the chef, however, took a penchant to Mahogany and the two of them would chew the fat while he prepared the musicians their free meal.

Mr. Olive's contract with the musicians stated clearly that they were to perform for ninety minutes on Monday and Saturday nights. Their compensation would be one free meal each, but a meal that was not more than five dollars on the menu, and absolutely no shrimp or salmon. They also received one Greek beer and, if supplies lasted, one almond cookie. Any other earnings would result from tips from the patrons which were to be tallied and reported each week.

Mahogany summoned the nerve to point out to Mr. Olive, "Sir, the only choices on the menu that cost five dollars or less are the appetizer of four dolmatas or a two-ounce souffle cup of tzatziki sauce."

Mr. Olive replied, reluctantly, "Oh alright, Ernest will select the five dollars' worth of food, but if I see you eating any shrimp, I'll take you to court."

While Mr. Olive scowled over his calculations in the bakery, Mahogany recounted his story to Ernest of how he departed Seattle and set his sails toward the Deep South after landing his first bona fide job, as an adjunct music professor at the Local Community College.

The quiet, wise, and full-muscled thirty-year-old Ernest had heard this story many times. Mahogany enjoyed the mysterious air that Ernest had, as if he knew things that no one else did. It made him an excellent audience because he seemed to understand, at a deep level, whatever anyone shared with him. Ernest listened amiably as he threw a handful of chopped onions, tomatoes, and green bell peppers onto the grill.

"It was through having a sense of humor, Ernest. There were seventy-eight candidates from all over the country competing for this position! And every last one of us had a Ph. D.! We only needed a bachelor's degree. These candidates graduated from good schools, too: Stanford, University of North Texas, Indiana University...everywhere. But they were too serious. That was their downfall," Mahogany observed.

Ernest added a dab of soy sauce and olive oil to the vegetables, making the grill hiss and steam. He wiped his brow which was perpetually coated in an annoying film of gyro grease which could only be successfully removed by employing straight white vinegar. He smiled in amusement at his friend's nerdiness, and affirmed, "It's true, bro. You is the funny man."

"But I'm also flexible," Mahogany elaborated in an unassuming humility. "And the other candidates were rigid. During my interview, the Dean of Instruction asked me if I was willing to teach other subjects besides the one advertised. They only needed a Music Appreciation instructor, but I offered to teach viola, bass, music theory, ethnomusicology, ear training, and the history of Rock and Roll. But you know what made him give me a second look? It was my published paper in the Journal of the American Musicological Society. Remember what it was about?"

By this point, Ernest was mixing in cube-sized chunks of pork into the souvlaki vegetables and sprinkling on the oregano and basil. "Uhh, something about sex, right?" he remembered.

"Yes! My paper was titled 'Sexual Discourse in the Parisian Chanson: A Libidinous Aviary,' and when I said that I was willing to teach a course based on my research, the Dean perked up."

Ernest, who had never finished high school while growing up in his native Pacific Island in Micronesia, and learned English as a second language, was too embarrassed to admit that he had no idea what Mahogany was talking about. His place in society back home on the tiny island in Micronesia required his brawn over brains, and the literary achievements of his friend were nothing short of baffling to him. But he had searched for some of these words on his smart phone, and reached the conclusion that anyone clever enough to defeat seventy-seven competitors by offering to teach college students how to have sex in a bird cage, had to be a cool guy, if not a little kinky.

"Once I could see that I had my foot in the door," Mahogany continued, "I shared a viola joke, and that was the feather in my cap. The job was mine!"

"Why is a viola like a lawsuit?" started Ernest. "Everyone is happy when the case is closed!"

They both laughed. Mahogany never got tired of the corny jabs that viola players endured.

Ernest inspected the sizzling pieces of chicken kebab that had been cooking over the charcoal flame, and with his bare fingers and without a flinch, slid them off the skewer and onto a plate. He dished a generous portion of basmati saffron rice to accompany it, and yelled out, "Order up!"

As Ernest contemplated how vastly different his world was from Mahogany's, he pulled out a steaming bowl of linguini from the microwave oven and handed Mahogany his meal of pasta with marinara sauce and shrimp topping. He garnished it with the final slice of Señora Conche's rejected pan dulce. Mahogany smiled as he took his free meal, unaware of how in the events to come, his friendship with the mysterious and buff Ernest would be what saves his life.

Malik, the prep cook, was perpetually accessorized with his white earbuds and was currently deriving immense pleasure from his playlist of Jay Z and Earth, Wind and Fire as he took fastidious care in shaving strips of lamb gyro off of the rotating vertical rotisserie cone. He was a large, gentle soul, donning a size 5x shirt, and had a propensity to ignore everyone unless he needed a fellow worker to give him a lift home when his shift concluded.

Malik also had a supplemental occupation as a bouncer at the Local Sports Bar. His head was never without the scrappy wool headband that held in place a nylon stocking that attempted to tame his seldom, if ever, washed hair that was half afro do and half dread locks that partly covered his eyes that stared out at the world in two different directions. His large head offset his enormous girth, and his shoes were slip on. Mahogany doubted that Malik had laid eyes on his own toes since he was in kindergarten. It stood to reason why he was employed as a bouncer given his intimidating physique. Malik merely had to threaten to sit on a troublemaker to keep them in line.

He lived in section 8 housing with his thirteen siblings, his mom, his grandmother, and two cousins. His mom was one of seventeen children, and most of her siblings lived next door or behind them in the same neighborhood, all within walking distance of the Local Greek Deli.

Despite the enormity of Malik's hands, he had acquired impressive fine motor skills for all tasks that involved chopping, slicing, or shaving things. He was quite proud of the fact that a video of him chopping six large onions into tiny pieces while he held them in his hand, in less than one minute, already tallied over three million views on YouTube. He declared himself as having attained Master Level, even though he had never attended a culinary school. Mr. Olive went along with it, and would sometimes boast to his customers that he had a master chef in the kitchen, assuming that possessing the skill to hew an onion into a million pieces in your hand without inadvertently severing a digit, met the criteria. Little did anyone at the Local Greek Deli foresee that Malik's skill with a knife would soon come in handy for more than just chopping vegetables.

Ernest informed the staff of the Local Greek Deli one day that in his native language of Micronesia, "Malik" translated to "chicken." This incited uproarious laughter.

Mahogany smiled at this, but offered an alternative. "Well, in Arabic, Malik means King."

"Awwww..." everyone reacted.

From then on, Malik was known as "King" at the Local Greek Deli.

King was most proficient at the art of shaving the perfectly thin gyro slice, from the beginning of the cone to the end. He swanked about how none of his gyro slices were tough like beef jerky, or thick and soggy, or thin and crumbly. He held out a large pan, displaying several pounds of his perfectly sliced gyro strips, offering them to Mahogany and pronouncing, "Now, that's what I'm talkin' about!" followed by his distinctive laugh "kee hee hee" that was reminiscent of Ernie from the *Muppet Show*.

Mr. Olive walked in from the bakery looking at the local

newspaper, and while pointing to a headline, he exclaimed loudly, "Look at that!"

King straightened himself more upright, displaying his gyro with more care, and responded, "Thank you, Mr. Olive, if I do say so myself."

Assuming that he had been caught red-handed, Mahogany reached in his pocket for his wallet, preparing to pay for the shrimp to avoid an appearance on the next episode of Judge Judy.

Mr. Olive said, "No, no. Look at this storm by the Leeward Islands. It's a Category 4! Hurricane Camille, predicted to make land fall directly on top of us this Friday!"

Scowling as he considered the consequences of 140 mph winds, he concluded, "I better tell Laquita that even if the Governor of South Carolina orders an evacuation of the entire city, she still has to show up for work. Or I'm taking her to court!" He huffed out of the kitchen to look for his AWOL employee.

"Where is Laquita, anyway?" asked Ernest. "I have five orders ready to go out. The food is getting cold."

King gave him a knowing look with a smirk.

"Oh, never mind," noted Ernest, as he recalled that when she placed the order for the chicken kebab about fifteen minutes earlier, Laquita was leading the guitarist, Valdimir, by the hand to the mountain stone granite storage shed. She winked at Ernest and claimed unconvincingly that they were procuring a fresh supply of Greek-style boneless, skinless chicken from the top-loading freezer.

The twenty-five-year-old single mom, Laquita Brown, held her true occupation as the head preschool teacher weekday mornings at the Local African Methodist Episcopal Church. She graduated cum laude with a Bachelor Degree in Elementary Education from the Orangeburg State College, and her nine-year-old son, Conner, was her young but dependable helper in the class. Her name at birth was Jane Margaret Brown Gist, and she determined as a youngster that she had a wastrel of a father, a certain States Rights Gist, V.

As part of her machination for retribution, she changed her name to disguise her identity when she arrived in the Port City of South Carolina where she knew he resided. Twenty-five years ago, her good-for-nothing father bedeviled one of his house servants, LaTonya Brown, with threats of terminating her employment if she refused his unwanted advances. He never acknowledged his paternal association when confronted with the news of LaTonya's pregnancy a few months later. Not once did the scoundrel offer a red cent to help LaTonya raise their child.

In the faint hopes that it would soften him, and perhaps someday bring her employer to recognize his paternity, the misemployed house servant, LaTonya, had named the baby girl Jane Margaret, after the wife of his great-great granddaddy, General States Rights Gist. But her efforts were bootless. The Fifth not once laid eyes on his first and only child, his bi-racial daughter, Jane Margaret Brown Gist, much less concede her existence.

Jane Margaret was aware that her father was a well-known elected official and author of white supremacist rhetoric, but she had only recently become savvy to the gossip that he struggled with an uncontrolled gambling habit. That's when the wheels in Jane Margaret's mind began to spin with vengeful fantasies, for learning to forgive was not on her bucket list when it came to her disreputable father, The Fifth. The only goal Jane Margaret had in her heart was humiliation. Public disgrace and mortification. She felt a rush of gratification each time she deliberated her ploy. But she also wanted money. Lots of it. So she spent months devising a plot to blackmail her racist parental unit, in front of the biggest audience possible. Securing a job as a waitress where his weekly poker game occurred, at the Local Greek Deli, was step one of her multifaceted plan. She knew that as long as she changed her name to Laquita, The Fifth would never realize who she was, and she could keep a close eye on him. She was implementing the old adage that says: "A wise person keeps their friends close, and their enemies even closer."

Vladimir thought he had died and gone to heaven. It didn't matter that he was only busking for tips and a meal, playing dinner music for the patrons of the Local Greek Deli. He would have labored for free, knowing that he had a regular hot-blooded rendezvous with Laquita in the granite storage shed on top of the freezer filled with Greek-style boneless, skinless chicken. "My god, she's on fire!" he would think and could hardly focus on the sheet music when she delivered food to the tables while he played his guitar. "She is the most gorgeous woman I have ever laid eyes on. And she likes me! Lord, I must have been a really good boy in a previous life," Vladimir concluded.

He was so mesmerized by her allure and tantalizing trips to the storage shed, that he would have leaped off of the enormous suspension bridge over the Port City River if she were to ever have made such an entreaty.

This is why Vladimir was not at all troubled when the storage shed door slammed shut behind him and Laquita, leaving them in the dark and trapped inside. Neither of them had secured the wooden bolt that kept the door from closing completely and latching the lock. There had been many employees who had inadvertently imprisoned themselves in the storage shed over the years, so no one dared to go fetch a new supply of boneless, skinless chicken without toting their cell phone, in the event that they would need assistance from a coworker to unfetter them. But this particular Monday evening, both Laquita and Vladimir had forgotten their cell phones, and upon the door slamming the bolt in place, they were unwittingly held captive in the darkness of the storage shed with the lurking green gecko and the Palmetto bug. However, they were too distracted to notice as they passionately disrobed and acrobatically positioned themselves precariously above the top-loading freezer.

Chapter 3

It became evident that it was of no consequence that Laquita had abandoned her waitressing duties and the food was waxing tepid. Mahogany tagged behind Mr. Olive to the dining room where he had left his viola hanging by its scroll from the lip of the Manhasset music stand. He well-nigh collided into Mr. Olive who had abruptly stopped in his tracks and was gaping in disbelief. The entire dining room was deserted. The Monday Night Regulars at the Local Greek Deli, all sixteen dining tables covered in blue table cloths laced in white and yellow trim, every one of the 23 people who arrived every week as predictably as Christmas decorations after Halloween, had disappeared, abandoning their meals in various states of consumption. The Regulars' purses, jackets, napkins, and phones were all sitting on the tabletops. King noticed that something peculiar was adrift, and stood at the swinging kitchen doors saying, "You be serious?!"

The Monday Night Regulars were not the type of people to vamoose their seats in a hurry or leave food behind, unattended. They had all come to know each other warmly over the years, and they enjoyed each other's company and predictable appearances at the Local Greek Deli. For instance, there was a certain lady named Annalisa, who took ten minutes to place her order, which she would only relay to Mr. Olive and no one else, even though it was the same food every week. She phoned ahead, every Monday afternoon at 5 p.m. to confirm that Mr. Olive was on the premises to dictate her order. She fancied her Greek salad with the feta cheese on the side. The salmon kebab was to be grilled in water, no oil, well done, but not tough. The hummus was to come with her glass of red wine, which was to be poured into a white wine glass, and with an extra slice of pita bread cut into eight triangles, not four. Mr. Olive would hang up the phone, shaking his head, and remark, "God makes all kinds of people."

Then there was the elderly couple Lee and Leigh, who had been married for sixty-two years, with three middle-aged children, Lee Jr., LeighAnn, and Leeroy, who required an entire ten minutes to waddle from the Deli entrance to their favorite spot at Table 13. Another five minutes lapsed in order to fold the walker and hang up the cane. Garth was the overqualified public defender, with three master's degrees, two Ph.Ds., and a Doctor of Jurisprudence, who would marinate at table twelve for five to six hours, drinking bottomless pitchers of Luzianne sweet tea and nibbling on a xoriatiki salad. His only discernible motion was to make tracks to the little boys' room every forty-five minutes. Otherwise, he was absorbed in his laptop, oblivious to the world around him. Mahogany wagered that if he were to bring a trombone and play right into Garth's ear, he would remain unperturbed.

The echoing silence of the dining hall with the half-eaten food made for an eerie scene. It was comparable to an archeological dig site from a city covered by a volcano blast, but without the lava, everyone caught mid-sentence, but without the people.

Mahogany could not imagine any reason for them to

have gone missing, and for a brief moment he considered the possibility of an alien abduction. Then he wondered if it had been his viola playing.

Mr. Olive, Mahogany, and King looked at one another all flummoxed, and in unspoken agreement, headed out in search of the Monday Night Regulars who had gone astray. Their quest was brief, for as soon as they passed through the entrance of the Local Greek Deli, they discovered the wayward customers, flocked together on the sidewalk, all facing the opposite side of the Local Main Avenue, which was bustling with rush-hour traffic. There, across the street, furniture shoppers of all monetary means could purchase wares at the Big Sofa Wholesale Store that occupied half of the city block.

As Mahogany looked in the direction of the iPhones that some of them were using to film the Big Sofa Wholesale Store, whimsically named "Shack of Sit" by the fun-loving jokester and proprietor, Mr. Marion, a man so sociable that he would talk to himself if no one else was handy, it became directly patent what circumstance was tragically betiding. A fire was ballooning into billowing black smoke towers, no less than twenty feet high, originating from behind the main showcase expanse, and foretelling an ominous outcome. As Mahogany considered whether to dial 911, he perused the crowd that had converged on the sidewalk, apparently with the same haste as the Monday Night Regulars. He recognized the neighboring storekeepers that had congregated along the Local Main Avenue.

Standing a few yards away was the tattoo shop owner, Sheila, a young woman activist for the LBGTQ community, who had paid her way through a Master's Degree in Social Work by painting portraits on canvas, and then decided to be an entrepreneur doing portraits on human skin. She stood there with her cordless tattoo gun in hand, next to her partially disrobed client who was sporting 40 percent of Donald Trump's face on his shoulder blade. Next to them was the shady fellow who peddled payday loans with questionable candor, and who was conveying an impuissant expression as he paced the sidewalk to and fro, wringing his hands, clearly distraught by the sight of the fire.

Scattered among them were Locals and tourists who were coincidentally happening by. Then, for a fleeting instant, Mahogany saw his Italian friend, Ferdinand Lombardini, the concertmaster violinist of the Local Symphony Orchestra, exiting the loading dock of the neighboring Tillman Auditorium, proceeding at a rapid clip into the crowd, and then making haste in a blur toward the direction of his house, which was located directly behind the Shack of Sit.

MarvLee Borman, the endearing and winsome 25-year-old of Gullah descent from Daufuskie Island, did not see the flames from the backstage area of the Tillman Auditorium when he cleverly cued Ferdinand Lombardini to sneak out through the loading dock exit. As the longest-serving union stagehand at the Port City's Local Performing Arts Center, MarvLee knew every nook and cranny of the building. He could draw a blueprint for all the backstage dressing rooms, stairways, green rooms, catwalks, and the recording booth that was accessible only by a thin iron ladder. It was his home away from home. As a part-time volunteer fireman, he knew the location of all the fire exits, and was aware of all the doors and windows that violated city codes.

MarvLee was also the only union stagehand of the Tillman Auditorium to mingle with a particular coterie of Local Symphony Musicians after concert performances, to relax and consume an illegal herbal substance from an infamous ceramic waterpipe christened "Chucho," which was a treasured possession of Ferdinand Lombardini. Everyone gave a wink and a nudge when the fun-loving, gregarious Ferdinand would invite the motley denizens of the orchestra to his humble abode across the street to make the acquaintance of his "little friend, Chucho."

MarvLee was always the life of the party at these regular gatherings, for he had an engrossing storytelling ability that he would spice up with his distinctive, unwonted humor. MarvLee had a special intrigue for the classical orchestra musicians because he was the youngest brother of the famous opera star sensation, Tessie Borman, which made him an irresistible source of celebrity gossip that mesmerized the stoned performers with rapt attention. Whenever his stories centered around his childhood and his beloved legendary sister, all bloodshot eyes were fixated on him.

"My big sister, Auntie Tee, we all call her," MarvLee would boast. "She was a saint. She was holy. Course, she had no choice but to be that way. Growing up on Daufuskie Island, intelligence be faster than any o dat cyber space mojo. If you did summit you shouldn't be doin on the North end of the island, by the time you reached the South end of the island only five miles away, by any mode of transportation, everbuddy already knew the sin you just done committed. And if every Sunday you didn't get to church by the last "holy" you was officially late. And you be feelin the eyes on your neck. And the worst thing to happen to you was to see your school teacher talking to your parents after church. You changed that red mark ("f") on your report card to blue fast!"

MarvLee would chuckle at his memories and inhale a fresh dose from Chucho, then pass it over to a compadre. After a long exhale, he would continue with the story seasoned and spiced with more of his quaint comments.

"You either sang in the church choir, or you ushered. You had a place, so you couldn't skip. You had to be strategic with your passes, on your Sundays you didn't show up. Our mom and dad, they were patriotic, religious and when they disciplined us, it was quiet but effective and deadly. If you dare to roll your eyes, and Mom or Dad ask 'Who you be rolling your eyes at?' you knew that nobody's name was the right answer."

MarvLee would scoop up a handful of popcorn from a bowl of snacks on the coffee table where several of the musicians always propped up their feet, waiting to hear more.

Someone inevitably would ask, "So, how is it that your big sister ended up being an opera star?"

"Here's the thing," he would reply, thoughtfully. "Yes, you was black. All you had to do was look in the mirror to know that. But what else was you gonna do? People think, black folk never sing in opera. But Auntie Tee didn't care. She wanted to sing. So she sang. Nothing mattered to her but that fancy singing. So she did it. I'm just glad she still comes home and takes a turn now and then to host Easter dinner, because when it's Auntie Tee's turn to host, you know that meant that food be lying everywhere. You be eatin for days."

And so it would go on into the wee hours.

Monday evening was MarvLee's customary shift to offer his services as a volunteer fireman in the picturesque Port City of South Carolina, a vocation that he found continually gratifying because of the exhilaration of saving the lives of the Port City Locals, and their three-hundred-year-old domiciles in the famous historic hamlet. Homes that survived centuries of hurricanes, cannon balls, and earthquakes could disappear in mere moments from a faulty electric wire catching fire. MarvLee was determined that it would never occur on his watch. His volunteer squad precinct held him in the utmost regard after he won the annual "Local Hero" medal award because of his expertise at rescuing cats from tall trees, an honor which he unabashedly used to procure several diverting dinner dates.

But due to a shuffling of schedules, MarvLee had traded shifts with a fellow fireman, which allowed him to take on the duties at his primary employment as a union stagehand. So, that fateful summer Monday in June, he left his protective uniform and gear at home, and dressed in a black long-sleeved T-shirt and black jeans. Instead of climbing fire truck ladders, he was climbing dangerous 30 foot high catwalks above the side theatre in order to aim very hot stages lights at very fragile egos for the monthly fundraising chamber concert at the Tillman Auditorium of the Local Performing Arts Center.

CHAPTER 4

At approximately 6:30pm, a scowling, dour FBI agent paid an unexpected visit. He entered the Tillman auditorium's main entrance and walked determinedly across the blue-carpeted foyer. He appeared nondescript, clothed in a dark blue suit that covered a white button-down shirt with no tie. Except for the gun holster barely concealed by the jacket, and the Ray-Ban balorama Men-in-Black sunglasses, one would not differentiate the agent from other audience members.

Unlike the other concert goers, however, Mr. FBI man did not appreciate the rococo architecture of the grandiose staircase that served as an ostentatious backdrop for wedding photo shoots, nor did he admire the finely sculpted marble statues of Confederate heroes lining the walls. The Baroque paintings of cherubs playing lutes for the Virgin Mary that adorned the ceiling did not impress the impatient federal operative. Nor did the soothing sounds of the Andante third movement of Brahms Piano Quartet in C Minor, opus 60 wafting from the side theatre stage, succeed in mollifying his mood. Mr. FBI man had only one undertaking imprinted on his mind, and he wanted to complete his assignment without delay in order to go home and enjoy a Scotch on the rocks while watching reruns of *American Ninja Warrior*.

He flashed his badge at MarvLee, who was enroute to the closet by the elevator which housed the extra spotlight LED bulb he needed in that moment.

"Why, yes, sir, how may I help you, sir?"

Mr. FBI man was clearly in a foul mood, and simply demanded to be escorted directly to Mr. Ferdinand Lombardini posthaste.

Being quick on his feet, MarvLee conjectured that his buddy was in a definite pickle. He knew that Ferdinand was presently tuning his violin to perform a Paganini Caprice for the fundraiser concert in progress. He was tightening the horsehair on his bow, adjusting the chinrest on the violin to fit under his neck securely and preparing to walk onstage and bend himself at the waist in a full bow to the audience. All this without a whiff of suspicion that he was about to encounter an unsympathetic bloke with a gun, who intended to escort him back off the stage without a single gallantry, and presumably into the backseat of a patrol car.

MarvLee knew that Mr. FBI man had arrived that Monday evening at the Tillman Auditorium of the Local Performing Arts Center for the purpose of apprehending and collaring Ferdinand for infractions of the law pertaining to plant-like narcotics and the consumption thereof. And with his agile mind, MarvLee responded, "Oh, you mean Chucho! Sure, absolutely, Mr. FBI man. I'd be much obliged to lead you right to him. He's a good friend of mine, ole Chucho. Love him to pieces. Here, step right this way. Chucho and I go way back. We met before my son was born, that's how far back we go, yes, siree."

And so began MarvLee's meandering tour through the corridors, galleries, and arcades of the old auditorium to buy himself time to concoct a means to warn Ferdinand to leave the building.

"Right this way, Agent."

They descended a flight of stairs next to the elevator and entered the costume shop.

"Anybody seen Chucho here as of late?" MarvLee called out.

He led the way through the piles of wardrobe changes for the upcoming production of Verdi's opera, "Aida." A popular work with a cast of a thousand, real live elephants and an operating budget the size of war.

MarvLee declared to the FBI agent, "Let me tell ya somethin' right now. No amount of union overtime be enough money for me to be cleanin' up no elephant dung. No way. Not me. Seriously? No. I ain't cleanin' up no elephant dung. That be the truth. Forget it. No way. No one be seeing me cleanin' up dat mess. Elephant dung? No. You be serious? No. Not me. No, siree. I ain't be doin' any o dat!" He shook his head emphatically at the thought of such a prospect.

The two men saw no one but the full-time seamstress sitting hunched over an electric Singer with an unlit cigarette hanging from her lip. She briefly raised her head to look at them with an annoyed expression, but said nothing. They ascended the staircase on the opposite end of the costume shop where they found a locked fire door clearly stating: "Fire Door. No Entrance."

"Why, I'ms so sorry, sir. I guess we needs to go an' backtrack to the fo-yay."

Once they arrived back at the blue carpeted foyer, and walked by the ossified, commanding General Robert E. Lee, MarvLee hailed Julia, a friendly usher for the fundraising recital that was about to present Ferdinand to the audience.

"Julia, have you seen Chucho?! This here fine FBI agent be looking for him."

Julia sensed the irony in MarvLee's voice and gave the grumpy scowler a once over. Calmly she informed them, "Chucho is in the upstairs rehearsal room practicing with the Gospel Choir."

As the two men ascended the elevator to the second floor,

MarvLee silently released a sigh of relief. Julia had understood. Her daughter, Amber, was the same age as Ferdinand and his late wife's two young lads. Julia admired Ferdinand's ability to entertain the children when they visited at the park every Monday. He could keep the brood shrieking joyfully for hours with cartwheels and riding horsebacks. The last thing Julia wanted was for Ferdinand to get into any unpleasantness with the law. She knew her Amber would be devastated if she couldn't spend her Monday afternoons with the boys.

The elevator doors opened on the second floor to the strident volume of a Hammond B3 Organ's flourish of notes, accompanying a soloist improvising on "When I Get in Glory" while the choir clapped in unison, swaying left, then right. The singer held a tambourine, tapping it in rhythm as she displayed vocal acrobatics that would have made Aretha Franklin proud.

Recognizing the opportunity to stall the agent, MarvLee immediately began clapping along, and joined in the choir's chant. "Everbuddy shout yeah yeah. Everbuddy shout!" He jerked his hips, and swung his shoulders back and forth, his eyes closed, and his head bobbed up and down enthusiastically, apparently overcome with the high emotion of praising the Lord.

Mr. FBI man, oblivious to the ecstasy of the music, rolled his eyes behind his black balorama glasses, and made three attempts before successfully landing the attention of the conductor who was gyrating and belting out snippets of laudation while using a large towel to wipe perspiration from his neck.

"Is Ferdinand Lombardini present?"

Without missing a beat, the gospel director kept the choir's energy climaxing while he pointed to the special elevator door leading to the concrete bunker bomb shelter, added to the Tillman Auditorium during the early years of the Cold War in 1950.

The windowless bomb shelter bunker was perpetually occupied by the Local Symphony Orchestra's Librarian, Oliver, who took his job very seriously. There was a cot in the back corner for the times when his workload piled up and he needed to work through the night. He prided himself with his superior professionalism in his craft.

However, no one on the Symphony staff, not the Executive Director, nor the Music Director, nor any of the Symphony Musicians; not the Operations Manager, the Personnel Manager, nor the Education Outreach Manager; not the Volunteer Coordinator, the Marketing Director, nor the Development Director; not his wife; and sadly not even his dog, had the remotest idea what Oliver did all day long.

All anyone knew for sure is that if Oliver failed to show up for work, then without question, everyone associated with the Local Symphony Orchestra of Port City, South Carolina, was sure to be screwed.

MarvLee and the FBI agent grunted as they heaved open the heavy bunker door made of iron, and came upon Oliver, surrounded by his usual tools consisting of several bottles of white and cream-colored correction white-out liquid, an electric eraser, several handheld erasers made of an assortment of materials, six-inch, twelve-inch and thirty-six-inch rulers, custom-ordered rolls of paper tape, a saddle stapler, black felt tip pens, and boxes of 2B pencils. They noticed the ever-present whirring sound of the seven thousand dollar Canon office copy machine that spit out sheet music non-stop 24 hours a day next to the wall that displayed a large sign warning of the current federal copyright laws pertaining to classical composers.

Oliver was inspecting the piccolo part to "Stars and Stripes Forever" and appeared satisfied with his work at cleaning up the excess pencil markings, making it easier to read. It did not carry persuasive import to the Local Symphony Orchestra Librarian that the Piccolo player had already tallied 748 performances of the oft-programmed piece, and could play it in her sleep. As Oliver blew small white eraser crumblings off of the music onto

.

a pile on the floor that had grown big enough to stuff a pillow, he asked how he could be of assistance.

Oliver suggested that Ferdinand must be backstage of the main Tillman concert hall stage, so MarvLee led the way out of the bunker, grateful for the extra moments to stonewall. As the door was closing behind them, Mr. FBI man assumed that the Librarian was a member of the armed forces, given that he was preparing a patriotic song, and said over his shoulder as they left the bunker, "Thank you for your service."

Oliver broke into a smile. That was the nicest thing anyone had ever said to him.

Twenty minutes after their excursion of detours began, MarvLee and the agent ended up backstage of the main concert hall, where a bass trombonist was warming up his instrument with long slow tones, rising and falling in volume, as if to mock an approaching and departing train.

"Say, have you seen Chucho? This FBI gentleman be looking for him," MarvLee asked in an unusual tone of voice.

The bass trombonist, silently and thoughtfully removed the brass slide from the bell, reached the full extent of his long arm, and opened the spit valve. He had a strong loyalty to Ferdinand ever since that day eight years ago when they were fishing off of the Local Waterfront Pier. While reaching over the railing to release a baby shark that he caught by mistake, he lost his bearing and fell into the ocean, and was taken swiftly away by a rip current. Ferdinand had spent his summers in college as a lifeguard for the YWCA, and without hesitation, dove in after his bass trombonist compadre. By the time Ferdinand swam to his friend, he had lost consciousness, so he had to hold and drag him to shore. Three different videos from nearby beachgoers were played on the Local TV News Stations for a week.

So, the bass trombonist stood backstage with the other two men, took his time joggling out the condensation that had accumulated in the instrument's metal slide, and created a small puddle on the floor, precariously close to the federal official's shoe. With an understanding nod, in a voice reflecting his unruffled disposition, he informed them, "Yes, Chucho is on the main concert hall stage, rehearsing with the full orchestra."

"Thank you, bro. we'll just have a short meeting with him by the loading dock," replied MarvLee with a wink.

The members of the Local Symphony Orchestra were in the main concert hall of the Tillman Auditorium in the midst of rehearsing Tchaikovsky Symphony No. 4. The Maestro was directing from the podium, offering his interpretation of the Romantic masterwork to his colleagues with hackneyed phraseology that was steadily leading the musicians into various states of mental torpor.

A few recalcitrant tenured musicians in the back of the ensemble, farthest from the conductor, were playing bingo as their director spoke. His well-worn verbiage made for a winner every hour.

"Make it sound like chamber music!" encouraged Maestro Ding as he waved the conductor's baton in circular gestures that failed to convey any discernible information.

"Make it sound like Brahms!" he continued. "I want strength, not volume! What's wrong with the bass section, do you all have low instrument disease?"

"BINGO! Ha ha!!" exclaimed the second chair bassoonist.

"Sir, Maestro Ding, I apologize for the intrusion. But this FBI agent be looking for Chucho," interrupted MarvLee.

The musicians eventually all stopped playing Tchaikovsky and making random doodling noises and rested their instruments on their laps. The oboist removed the reed from the reed socket of the upper joint and began blowing high-pitched rapid duck calls through it to determine if he wanted to switch to another one of the 57 reeds that he had in his briefcase.

Eventually, all heads turned to the stage-left curtains where the two men stood. A prolonged silence ensued, as no one wanted to speak up, thereby admitting that they knew the code word for the infamous waterpipe. Finally, the Assistant Concertmaster summoned the courage to reveal his membership in the club, and elucidated, "Chucho took a personal day off today. That's why I'm sitting first chair."

The bass trombonist, seeing that Mr. FBI man was occupied, dashed away and quickly located Ferdinand exiting the Ravenel Theatre stage on the opposite side of the foyer. The applause was still going strong, and Ferdinand was about to acknowledge their appreciation of his performance of Paganini's Caprice No. 24 with another bow, but instead the bass trombonist grabbed his elbow, informing him with urgency, "Amigo, the feds are here searching for you on the main stage as we speak. They know about Chucho! They're going to bust you for possession! You need to get the hell out of here fast! MarvLee told me that the safest way to get out is through the loading dock!"

Ferdinand was startled, but trusted his friend who had never stopped thanking him for saving his life, all these years later. He realized he didn't have time for his post-recital ritual of playing a four-octave scale in double-stop sixths. He quickly, but carefully, handed over his Villiaume violin dated 1860, removed his bow tie, threw it on the floor, and disappeared into the costume shop.

He ran past the Verdi wardrobe and the unlit cigarette, up the stairs with the door clearly labeled "Fire Door. No Entrance," pushed it open, ran into the men's dressing room's left entrance, ran out of its right entrance, then rushed through the percussion storage room where he paused behind the biggest timpani kettledrum to peek around the corner and see if the coast was clear.

He saw MarvLee discreetly motioning with his left hand toward the loading dock while Mr. FBI man continued interrogating the musicians of the Local Symphony Orchestra. He saw the Maestro checking his vacillating baton beats against his clicking metronome that was forever sitting on the conductor music stand. Seeing the opportunity to reach the exit, he stealthily escaped through the double wide roll-up loading dock door that was positioned half-way open.

As he darted onto the Local Main Avenue and merged into the crowd, for the first time Ferdinand saw that the Shack of Sit, a building directly adjacent to his home's backyard, was engulfed in flames. He repeated a few Hail Marys as he ran home to make sure that his mother, Nonna, his two boys, Julia's daughter, Amber, and MarvLee's son, Conner, who were always at their house on Monday nights were safe.

Like greased lightning, Ferdinand tore into his living room, snapped up Chucho from the top of the television set in the entertainment center and took wing into the music room where he hastily shoved aside his tripod and video camera that were blocking his oversized black canvas duffle bag where several VHS videos were stored. He crammed the infamous waterpipe to the bottom of the bag, underneath dozens of tapes. And in a blink of an eye he hid the oversized black canvas duffle bag in the cedar storage chest that was filled with strongly aromatic cedar chips.

As he grabbed his laptop and raced out of his house, little did Ferdinand know that the fading strains of Paganini Caprice No. 24 that were still lingering in the air of Tillman Auditorium would soon become his swan song.

Chapter 5

Laquita threw her head back in delight and reached back with her left hand to maintain her balance, only to feel something very odd. Rough material and something that felt like hair. Startled, she let out a scream, which sent Vladimir in a rocket ship to the moon. As he settled down, and slid off of the top-loading freezer to zip up his pants, Laquita fumbled for her cell phone to illumine the storage shed and see what she had touched, only to discover that she had left her phone inside the Local Greek Deli next to the kebab grill.

"Vladimir, do you have your cell phone?"

They could only feel each other breathing in the dark, listening to the gecko repositioning itself in the hinge.

"No," he said. He left it next to his guitar.

No cell phones, and the door was locked tight as a drum. Their pounding fists, their cries for help, to let them out, to hasten or they would perish of heat stroke, were all in vain. For not a soul remained inside the Local Greek Deli. Even Mr. Ernest had joined the gawking crowd on the front sidewalk, leaving the restaurant deserted, with no one left to hear them shouting in the back parking lot. Soon, the wails of the fire engines and police sirens would completely drown out their pleas.

"Vladimir, what did I touch? Is this a body?"

He dug into his pocket and found his cigarette lighter. For the first time, he was thankful for his nicotine habit, as he used his little Bic to illuminate the storage shed which was becoming hotter by the minute, in spite of them cooling off their passions.

There, behind the top-loading freezer was an enormous black canvas bag about three feet wide at the bottom and six inches wide at the top, with long strands of hair, a half a meter in length, mostly black, some white, thick, straight and dangling from a zipper near the middle. Laquita noticed that something sticky was on her fingers after having touched it. Their eyes widened in horror.

"We have to find a way out of here!" Laquita exclaimed. "There must be a loose board or something."

Soon, Christmas decorations, styrofoam plates, old spatulas, dead spiders, and live Palmetto bugs were flying through the air in all directions as they frantically searched for an alternate escape route.

"Here! I found something!"

Vladimir reached for an iron ring on the floor and, with great effort, pulled up a trap door that led to darkness below. Vladimir and Laquita stopped as they panted, wiping their brows, and considered the situation.

"How is it that we have never noticed this trap door before?" asked Vladimir, rhetorically.

The hour was now 7:00 p.m. and the Monday Night Regulars of the Local Greek Deli had watched the fire leap across the alley behind the Shack of Sit and begin to devour the enormous showcase room. The main display room was overladen with sofas, recliners and upholstered chairs arranged in an indecipherable, harrowing labyrinth of attenuated pathways. Pathways so complicated and perplexing that the owner, Mr. Marion, required his employees to dare not venture into them without being accompanied by a GPS tracking device.

The pathways were so perilous, in fact, that all employees were trained to recognize muffled cries for help when overly rotund customers became trapped into the folds of sofa cushions. It was rumored that an unknown number of hapless furniture shoppers had never vacated the main show room of the Big Furniture Wholesale Store.

As the tourists, Locals, and store owners looked on with horrid fascination from across the Local Main Avenue, the fire strengthened and migrated to the leather sofas that were precariously placed against the back wall, ten rows across, and stacked five high. The cushion fillings of polyurethane foam provided a fuel more formidable than pure gasoline, and due to the close proximity of the labyrinth of sofas, within moments, the flames consumed several other stacks of sofas.

The heat inside the main room of the Shack of Sit elevated almost instantaneously to temperatures so powerful that the roof truss fractured along its entire length. This caused a breach in the metal roofing, inviting massive flames to burst through and shoot up a hundred feet. The Monday Night Regulars of the Local Greek Deli all gasped in unison.

Sheila, the Tattoo artist cried, out, "The gas station!"

Only fifty meters away from the Shack of Sit was a Local Corner Gas Station with five fuel pumps and a large diesel tank. Suddenly, a wave of fear gripped over the spectators as they all imagined the worst.

"Where the hell are the goddamned fire trucks?" yelled the pacing payday loan shyster of questionable candor. "Didn't anyone call 911?"

Mr. Olive noted that the fire must have started at 6:50pm.

He had acquired the habit of checking the time whenever a moment of distress occurred during the medical treatment of his little Zorika. The nurses at Zora's medical retreat for children asked Nazoon if he would be so kind as to watch the clock and jot down the duration of her grand mal seizures that were taking place with more frequency.

He checked his watch again; it was now 7:10 p.m. and not one fire engine had arrived yet. No one could fathom what could have caused the delay. There were ten fire stations within a two-mile radius of the Local Greek Deli, and yet the absence of any siren was unbearable.

What the fine people of Port City, South Carolina, did not know was that the Local Firemen of the entire county were celebrating the retirement of one of their own with a catered retirement party that included an oyster roast and open bar at a Local Historic Plantation fifteen miles away. Not one single fireman was receiving the frantic messages of the 911 operators. Instead, they were wassailing in ignorance of the Shack of Sit's peril.

Mahogany couldn't bear watching anymore, and returned to the Local Greek Deli and sat nervously by his viola. He felt too unsettled to sit idly, so to keep busy, he started distributing styrofoam carryout containers to the deserted tables of the Monday Night Regulars. As he did so, Councilman States Rights Gist and Maestro Ding entered the Local Greek Deli through the side door labeled for emergency only, as they did each week, and loitered near their customary spots at Table 16 for their Monday night poker game.

Mr. Olive returned from the sidewalk and sat at his spot. After taking a few deep breaths, Nazoon asked his friends, "Did you not notice the Shack of Sit? It's on fire!"

The Local City Councilman responded, "That's a shame. I would surmise then, that Mr. Marion will be otherwise occupied tonight, and not playing cards with us."

"No, he won't," said Mr. Olive. "I will need to find a substitute player for this evening. But I tell you, if this fire makes my business suffer the loss of even one gyro sandwich sale, I'm going to take Mr. Marion to court!"

CHAPTER 6

Mr. Olive had accumulated the names of his poker associates on his speed dial, in the order of which person was most likely to be free on Monday nights. This allowed him to find substitute players on a moment's notice. The name positioned at the top of the assemblage of fellow gamblers that fateful Monday night was Dr. Gamble, the Local Transgender Surgeon of Port City who performed over 1,000 surgeries each year on the delicate tissues of no-longer-to-be male clients at the Local Medical University, affording him and his wife constant excursions abroad, among six continents. Each month, the couple ventured everywhere from points in the mid Pacific hugging the equator to desolated areas located within the Arctic Circle.

He was a huge man whose amiability matched his size, trailing his loose joints over a vast extent of territory. By the time the poker games entered the drinking phase, Dr. Gamble tended to make more wind than sense, and he would make embarrassing remarks in a booming voice that could be heard all the way out to the granite stone storage shed.

Upon Dr. Gamble's arrival at the Local Greek Deli, The Fifth, in a manner decidedly gruff and crusty, initiated events by moving a large photograph framed in heavy glass of Mr. Olive's heroes, Aristotle and Jackie Onassis, portrayed strolling hand in hand along the Beach of Skorpios Island. The photo hung above Table 16, serving as a cover for the inlaid shelves that stored all the necessary paraphernalia used for the weekly card game.

States Rights Gist first removed from the shelves a leather-bound book. He then removed a white handkerchief from his double-breasted jacket, carefully opened it, and flattened it onto a chair. And with the same gentleness as if it were a newborn, The Fifth placed the book on the chair, and made sure that its title "The Constitution" printed in 30 point font on the cover, was strategically within plain view of all participants. The deciding document was to be easily accessible for reference to determine the rules of any poker plays that were challenged, and whereupon any verbiage read from it would be stated with finality and tremendous oath.

Because the Monday Night Poker Game at the Local Greek Deli yoked the qualities of lawfulness and combat between equally addicted gamblers, it took over three months to find an arbiter to pen the contents of The Constitution, for it needed to be someone whom everyone agreed possessed the requisite wisdom and credentials as evidenced by lifelong dealings with high level matters of justice and morals.

The author of The Constitution ultimately selected was Lieut. Larry Derryberry, the tenured Sol Bratt, Jr. Professor of Jurisprudence and Public Policy at the Local Port City College of Law. Lieut. Derryberry's assignment in composing The Constitution was to protect the Monday Night Poker Players from each other's possible elastic ethics or murky forthrightness that could create suspicion. The Constitution was to cover as many thorny situations as could reasonably be imagined occurring during a round of Seven-card stud.

Maestro Ding was not concerned with all these formalities pertaining to The Constitution. He was relieved to just be done with the afternoon rehearsal of the Local Symphony Orchestra, and the interrogations of the surly FBI agent. He was looking forward to enjoying some baklava and a shot or two of ouzo as his dessert following a plate of lamb gyro souvlaki.

He did not particularly care for the fellow gamblers, but they made for an adequate captive audience for his long-winded pontifications and self-crowing. Maestro Ding tolerated the Local City Councilman, in spite of the fact that States Rights' extreme political views had won him odium from the sensitive, left-leaning, musical artist.

As a New Yorker, Maestro Ding considered himself much more refined in his high degree of European cultural breeding compared to the racist lowbrow Southerner, and seldom spoke to him directly, for he refused to be cajoled, in any manner, by the attentions of an electioneering backward politician.

The Maestro checked the position of his dark purple wool French beret in the reflection of the Greek shipping tycoon's glass frame, and being satisfied, he began his routine, for he was not without a sense for the dramatic, whereupon he reposed his Gucci cocoa leather ankle boots sublimely on an empty chair at Table 16 while he chatted in an easy vein about the niceties of life to convey a particular mode of reflection that he believed elevated his understandings in the eyes of anyone who happened to be listening.

The first order of business delineated by The Constitution, to avoid any player perceiving that they were being deliberately put at a disadvantage, was to randomly determine the evening's seating arrangement with a computer application installed on the iPad which was located on the inlaid shelves next to the cards and chips.

Upon the iPad displaying the current seating order, Dr. Gamble tipped his crocheted raffia fedora hat and nodded his head in the direction of each of his comrades before taking his chair. The Fifth responded with a tip of his linen pinstriped navy-blue trilby hat as he made himself comfortable next to the wall. Mr. Olive tugged impatiently at the front of his Greek fisherman's cap. And the Maestro brushed his hand delicately over his precisely placed French beret, so as not to disturb its position. The hats served as proud emblems of their heritage and sovereignty, but The Constitution required that everyone politely acknowledge that each man's own doctrine of transmitted instincts and peculiarities were not superior to the rest.

Mr. Olive then declared, "According to The Constitution, I determine the ending time for tonight's game. Since I have to be by Zoraki's side at seven tomorrow morning, we will stop at midnight sharp."

The Fifth chimed in, "In accordance with The Constitution, I determine today's table stakes. The first two hands will be ten dollars and two pieces of baklava, then no limit for the succeeding hands."

Hearing no objections, Mr. Olive rolled out a cart of mini pieces of baklava from the bakery reduced in size by half, but with the prices inflated three-fold from the menu listing.

Dr. Gamble pulled out the two decks of cards from the shelf and mulled over whether to use the plain nondescript blue deck or the red Greek deck that portrayed classic images of ancient mythological Greek lovers. The erotic deck was normally left concealed behind the image of the Greek billionaire's private island until after the Deli's closing time when there was no chance of offending a Monday Night Regular. As he studied the pretzeled contortions of Aphrodite and Athena entangled in a parlous threesome with Ares, he noticed that he was not hearing dinner music from Mahogany and Vladimir.

"Say, where is everyone?" he asked as he realized the place was empty.

"What, you didn't notice that the Shack of Sit is on fire?"

answered Mr. Olive. "It's only a hundred-foot flame. Are you blind?"

Dr. Gamble defended himself, "I drove in from the opposite direction. Is that why you called me, to fill in for Mr. Marion? I didn't see any fire trucks outside, nor did I hear any sirens. And is that why Mahogany's viola is hanging from the music stand?"

In all the excitement, Mr. Olive had momentarily forgotten about the dinner music normally provided to accompany the Monday Night Poker Game at the Local Greek Deli. And since Dr. Gamble had already started dealing the first cards, he decided to look for Mahogany after the first hand was finished.

Mahogany had sent several texts to his fellow musician Vladimir, to affirm his well-being and whereabouts, but he soon realized that the guitarist's phone was sitting in the open guitar case. He picked up his friend's phone and swiped through it to text Laquita, only to hear her phone sounding by the kebab grill. Suspecting that their romantic adventures had resulted in their imprisonment in the granite stone storage shed with the notorious top-loading freezer, Mahogany set out to release them.

As he stepped out through the back door of the Local Greek Deli and into the parking lot, he didn't know why, but he sensed an ominous mood as he approached the storage shed door that was shut tight. His breathing became shallow and he had doubts as to whether it was such a good idea to look for his friend. Maybe he took Laquita to his house, he reasoned. Despite his trepidation, Mahogany slowly slid the wooden bolt up and over the latch that had held the love-birds captive a short while earlier, and cautiously pulled open the door with a more-than-slight feeling of dread. As he peered inside, a plastic Santa Claus with a dead spider in its spun cotton beard rolled out and landed on his foot.

On top of some old spatulas and styrofoam plates on the floor he saw Mr. Olive's myrtle wood hand-carved walking stick lying abandoned. Next to that, he scratched his head as he deciphered that he was seeing an open but empty rifle storage case. Not knowing that it was the case for The Fifth's recently stolen Anschutz 1781 rifle, Mahogany surmised that Vladimir and Laquita were engaged in risky wholehearted roleplaying that he would rather know nothing about.

"Those two are so raunchy," he opined.

Seeing that his friends were nowhere at hand, and unable to shake the strong foreboding that something sinister was nearby, he returned to the dining area of the Local Greek Deli.

Careful to not disturb the gamblers, Mahogany quietly took his seat, lightly plucked the four strings on his instrument to check their tuning, tightened the horse tail hair on the bow, and began playing a transcribed cello suite by J. S. Bach for solo viola. About twenty measures into the Prelude of Suite No. 3 in C Major, Mr. Olive inquired, "Where is Vladimir?"

Mahogany found a cadence point before lifting his bow and lowering the viola onto his lap and responded, "I checked around; I even looked in the storage shed, but I did not see him. His phone is here. I assume he is outside with the crowd watching the fire."

Hearing that someone had just recently been in the storage shed, The Local City Councilman coughed involuntarily, took his second handkerchief from his pants pocket, and began to dab at drops of perspiration forming on his forehead.

"I noticed something odd though," continued Mahogany.

The Fifth dropped a card on the table, revealing an ace of hearts. "Something odd, eh? What do you mean, young lad?" The Fifth inquired, trying to conceal his shaky syntax.

"Well, I saw the myrtle wood walking stick on the floor. I wasn't sure why it was there. Mr. Olive, would you like for me to go get it for you?"

Before Nazoon could reply, The Fifth abruptly dropped all his cards face down onto Table 16, and said, "I'll go get it! You just keep playing that high falutin music."

States Rights hurried as fast as his eighty-year-old frame

would allow to the parking lot, hoping to find his stolen rifle as well as to make sure his secret was not exposed. His shoulders were tight and high up next to his ears as he opened the door to the mountain granite stone storage shed. He sighed and relaxed when he saw that the large black canvas bag had moved only slightly from behind the top-loading freezer and was still mostly concealed from view.

He looked down and saw on top of a pile of styrofoam plates the walking stick next to his empty rifle case. "Damn," he thought, "I loved that rifle. But I can't report it stolen since I got it as a gambling prize."

Resigned to the loss, he scooped up both items, tossed the empty rifle case into the back of his Dodge truck before returning to the game to hand his Greek friend his walking stick. Before entering the side emergency exit of the Deli to return to the card game, States Rights looked over at the Shack of Sit, assuming that the fire would have been extinguished by now. But that is not what the Local City Councilman saw as he goggled in disbelief.

CHAPTER 7

It was now 7:10 p.m., twenty minutes after the Monday Night Regulars had first called 911, and only one fire truck had arrived at the Shack of Sit. Only one lone fireman was manning the single truck, and he was frantically connecting a fire hose to a fire hydrant, even though he knew that it was too small for the current circumstances. The camera crews of the Local TV Stations had already begun to arrive and were setting up spots for filming, aiming the lens for the best angle to get the reporter's face and the entire height of the flames in the same frame.

Finally, at 7:20 p.m. the Locals, tourists, and the Monday Night Regulars could hear the sirens of thirteen fire trucks. They stepped back as the huge vehicles tore onto the scene and came screeching to a halt in front of the conflagration which was now visible from miles away. Not far behind were police cars and ambulances speeding to the emergency.

The Local Fire Chief, Monte McGee, an affable, heavy-jowled 53-year-old man of wholesome accomplishment, looked out from the front seat of his fire engine at the mushrooming inferno and began to utter earnest curses.

Mr. Marion had texted the Chief a floor plan of the warehouse while he was enroute from the retirement party at the popular Local Historic Plantation fifteen miles away. A party that he would regret hosting for the rest of his days on earth.

Unfortunately, the blueprint of the Shack of Sit did not heed a warning that a map for the labyrinth of furniture was also required to guide his firemen. The plan also lacked another crucial detail that would prove to be life-altering, that a steel truss system supported the roof over the massive showroom.

And yet another stroke of misfortune to be piled on Chief McGee's grey head was that the Local Fire Chief did not know that this very steel truss system located in the Big Sofa Wholesale Store, an architectural design known in the firefighting world as "widow maker" because it creates concealed spaces where fire can grow undetected and can collapse within twenty minutes, had already been melting in a sea of flames for thirty minutes.

The Local Fire Chief wasted no time and immediately ordered the Battalion Chief and the two most senior firemen to enter the building. They dutifully obeyed the command, bravely opening the front doors as they disappeared into the dense masses of whirling smoke.

Chief McGee then ordered five men to the rear entrance to the point of origin, where they came upon great flurries of roaring and crackling debris. At the corner of the block, the firemen in charge of connecting the hoses to the hydrant were muttering incivilities as they realized that the water pressure was insufficient to have a punishing effect on the colossal blaze.

Inside the warehouse, even though the rays of the setting sun were still illuminating a clear blue sky outside, the toxic black smoke made it dark as night. It was evident to the three men that had entered the main showroom, that the fire-resistant qualities that the sofas boasted on their cushion labels were purely theoretical.

From inside the Shack of Sit, the Battalion Chief radioed to his commander, "It's a maze in here, and visibility is zero."

CHAPTER 8

MarvLee waved cheerfully to the security desk officer as he left his job for the evening as the top union stagehand at the Tillman Auditorium. He headed over to retrieve his son, Conner, from across the street at Ferdinand and Nonna's house. MarvLee's heart swelled in gratitude for the Lombardinis' generosity to care for his son every Monday afternoon, gratuitously, since he was a baby, when he had been appointed joint custody of him with his mother, Jane Margaret. Young Conner was now nine years old, and had grown up with the two Lombardini sons, Matteo and Dante. The three boys bonded as if they were brothers and regarded Amber, Julia the usher's daughter, as their sister. Conner and Amber had grown into the habit of addressing Ferdinand as their "Babbino," their second papa.

MarvLee was feeling optimistic that he had parried Mr. FBI man sufficiently long enough for Ferdinand to stash the incriminating waterpipe. He sauntered along, whistling "nothin could be finer than to be in Carolina" in a relaxed and contented mood as he crossed the street from the Local Performing Arts

Center to the Lombardinis' home. He was feeling tickled with himself at his cleverness to fool a federal agent and entertaining himself recalling the annoyance on the operative's face when he was dancing to the gospel choir music.

But no sooner had MarvLee stepped off the curb than his tuneful melody abruptly drifted off mid phrase as he noticed the commotion of the emergency vehicles and the billowing flames of the sofa store. Immediately, concern for his friend who had switched shifts with him that Monday night surfaced, and he wondered if one of the figures in full gear that he saw running toward the warehouse was him. He knew that he must ask Nonna to care for Conner, to allow him to help his colleagues battle the alarming inferno.

He tapped on the front door, then used his key to enter the Lombardinis' house. Conner rushed up to give his dad an enthusiastic embrace that only a child can demonstrate unabashedly.

"Daddy, Daddy! I love you!"

"I be lovin you, too, Son." MarvLee patted him on the head, as he inspected the entertainment center to see if Chucho had been adequately concealed from the authorities.

He lifted Conner high, then twirled him upside down, held tight to his ankles, and began walking with him head down. Conner giggled in delight, wrapping his arms around his father's knees to stifle his walk. MarvLee called out, "It's me, Grandma Nonna. You here?"

He discovered her in the music room, sitting in front of a video monitor clearly disturbed by what she was viewing. "You ok, hun?"

She was silent for a moment, then instructed the boy in feigned cheerfulness, "Conner, go play with your brother fratellos. Close the door, your father and I need some privacy."

Her pained expression directed MarvLee's gaze to the tripod and video camera. They were positioned next to the chest topped with cedar chips where the black duffle bag filled with VHS videos was serving to conceal Chucho. The waterpipe was surrounded by dozens of videos so that only its mouthpiece could be seen.

Nonna explained, "Ferdinand came running in here like a bat out of hell saying that the FBI was looking for Chucho. He threw the pipe in here. Then he left the house as fast as he came."

She paused. It was evident that the video was distressing. "So I came in here to make sure he hid it completely."

Tears began to form as her voice quavered. "MarvLee, I swear to God, I have never once, not ever, looked at these videos. The only reason I even gave them a second glance today was because I saw that one was labeled 'Amber, Lesson 5.'"

She began to choke on her tears. "MarvLee, Amber doesn't take violin lessons from Ferdinand. These are not videos of music lessons."

MarvLee suddenly felt awash in uneasiness, and the color drained from his face. He slowly approached the monitor where Nonna sat, her face pallid, and stepped around the desk beside her. There on the screen was Amber, Julia's daughter, appearing to be four years old, playing the violin while dressed in a little girl's bikini. Amber was listening to Ferdinand, who could only be heard, giving her instructions, "Tiny little alligators. Tiny little alligators," while the little girl moved a miniature violin bow, mimicking the rhythm of the words.

MarvLee and Nonna looked at each other, speechless. Each was feeling punched in the gut, overwhelmed with a vast array of unexpected and unwanted emotions. The sense of betrayal, horror, and desire for vengeance deluged them. Then they both looked over at the duffle bag filled with what looked to be nearly a hundred videos surrounding Chucho.

Nonna wondered out loud, "How many lessons did he give Amber?"

This led MarvLee to exclaim in alarm, "What if they be

videos of Conner?"

He tripped over the tripod, knocking it over as he desperately clenched the duffle bag, sending the ceramic waterpipe crashing to the floor and shattering it to pieces. As he crushed pieces of ceramic under his feet, he hastily rummaged through the bag, and quickly found a VHS video labeled "Conner Lesson 11."

MarvLee brusquely pushed Nonna aside, and hurriedly exchanged videos. His fingers trembled as he pushed the play button. The screen cruelly revealed a video of Conner with all of his youthful mocha skin exposed as he danced to various children's songs that Ferdinand was playing on the violin, exposing his innocence to the concealed camera lens. Horrified, MarvLee grabbed the video out of the machine.

"This is why dat FBI man be looking for Ferdinand! Almighty God of the Lord on high!! Chucho was nuttin to do with it!" He wailed and shook his head in the palms of his hands.

They stopped, frozen, looking at each other, completely shocked and outraged. MarvLee was overcome with an impulse to ambush Ferdinand if occasion offered.

He demanded to know, "Where's dat Ferdinand? I swear he's gonna regret the day he was born!"

"I don't know!" Nonna cried. "He ran out the door about twenty minutes ago."

MarvLee declared, "I be takin' all these nasty videos right now and rippin' 'em apart. I ain't be lettin' nobody, no FBI, no police, I said nobuddy, see my chile with no clothes on! They ain't be none o dat, you hear?!"

Nonna stood helpless and dumbstruck as MarvLee gathered all the videos into the oversized black duffle bag, zipped it closed, and flung it over his shoulder. His former plan to allow Conner to stay a few more hours as he fought a fire was determinedly, resolutely, and permanently altered.

CHAPTER 9

It had been an hour since Ernest watched the lovebirds through the Deli's kitchen window disappear into the storage shed. At this point, Vladimir was guiding the way down the wooden ladder underneath the trap door, and then through the dark secret tunnel beneath the granite storage shed of the Local Greek Deli. He was mystified that no one had ever revealed the existence of the underground channel. Did Mr. Olive know about this?

He tried to maintain his focus so as not to slip on the slimy surface underfoot. He carried his cigarette lighter high in one hand, and clasped Laquita's trembling hand in his other. He noticed that her fingers were still sticky from touching the hair that was dangling from the oversized black canvas bag and shuddered as he considered what it might be. A ray of light was slightly discernable several yards away through what appeared to be a storm shelter entrance.

The air was damp, the stone walls of the tunnel were covered in moss, and the fetid smell of South Carolina coastal pluff mud was overwhelming.

"Hurry up, Vladdy. Let's get out of here!" Laquita urged, lowering her head to avoid touching the clammy ceiling with her hair.

Despite being spooked into a cold sweat, she was certain that if her nine-year-old son, Conner, were there with them now, he'd be thrilled at the adventure. He was the only child she knew who eagerly anticipated gallivanting through haunted houses. She loathed the thought, and would recruit his father, MarvLee, to accompany him to the Old City Jail's annual spook house every October.

Soon, they both arrived at the source of light, and looked up at five steeply inclined stairs leading to two wooden horizontal doors. "Please, Lord, don't be locked," prayed Laquita.

Vladimir was about to ascend the stairs when he noticed an open door to the side of the tunnel that revealed a small wooden table with a dimming flashlight resting on it. "Hey, what's in there?" asked Vladdy with piqued curiosity. "Maybe this is where the ghosts of the Old City Jail live!" he speculated only somewhat in jest.

"Oh my God, who cares? Let's get out of here now!" Laquita replied in exasperation, pulling at his sleeve.

Vladimir couldn't resist the mysterious allure of the unattended beaming flashlight, and abandoned Laquita by the steps, assuring her, "I just want to see why this flashlight is on."

The room was small, but there was another doorway on the opposite side. He grabbed the flashlight and thumped it against his palm to encourage a brighter charge from the battery. He directed the beam to illuminate the doorway, and could see nothing posing as a threat, so he peered through the ingress. He walked through, and began to cautiously descend a lengthy concrete stairway, He held his breath as he placed his foot on each step, hoping that it wasn't slick with moss and causing him to fall. Holding firm to the handrail, he slowly reached the bottom, then waved the flashlight in a sweeping motion around and gasped in amazement.

"What! What? What do you see, Vladdy? Come back, let's go!" cried Laquita from the top of the stairs.   But what Vladimir saw was much more captivating than his lover's pleas.

Vladimir discovered that there was an enormous cavern, with stalagmites and stalactites punctuating a narrow shallow stream that divided a gravel floor, with walls at least thirty feet tall. He had visited caverns like this in the North Carolina mountains, but was unaware that they existed as far south as Port City. As he took a step forward, his head hit a hanging cord with a workman's incandescent hand lamp hanging from it. He switched it on and stood motionless. The first thing to become visible was a portentous 1781 Anschutz rifle propped against the banister railing.

This left him feeling unnerved, but he couldn't resist the urge to explore what he saw in the walls. Arranged in long straight rows, hundreds of ancient small boxes with the names of men engraved sloppily on rusty, metal labels had been inserted into the stone surface. It took the guitarist a moment to decipher, but he soon realized that this was a mausoleum potter's field, no doubt for the prisoners of the Old City Jail. He came upon an enclave in the wall with remnants of iron gate rods protruding out of each side. He saw some type of hieroglyphics, and as he examined them more closely, he deduced that this had served as a solitary confinement cell, and the markings were the captive person's way to keep track of the days. His heart began to pound. He could hear Laquita begging him to return. But he wanted to investigate what he saw on the far end of the cave.

Six long, narrow, multi-leveled metal shelves were lined along the cave wall displaying row upon row of Tupperware storage bins. He peeked inside several of them. They were filled with manilla envelopes, fake shipping labels, and mounds of white pills. Forged signatures on counterfeit prescriptions pads prescribing surfeit doses of oxycodone and oxycontin. Hundreds of Narcon emergency packs were in one of them.

Vladimir realized in dismay that he had stumbled onto a distribution center for illicit pain killer medicine. He understood that these ostensible magic bullets could catapult an entire populace into tumult, even the refined town of Port City, South Carolina, was not immune. An operation such as this, in a hidden catacomb underneath the Old City Jail, was a minor, yet dangerous contribution to the unintended demise of an entire population. He felt anger and apprehension simultaneously. He wanted to clobber whoever was answerable to these sinister going-ons.

He considered waiting for the culpable parties to return to the cavern so as to give them a piece of his mind. He would tell them how his youngest brother succumbed to these pills even after herculean efforts to save him in rehab. As he recalled the awfulness he felt that day five years previous when he discovered his brother lying on the kitchen floor, lifeless from countless imprudent overdoses, he got himself worked up into a tiff, ready for confrontation. But the intimidating Anschutz 1781 rifle that was positioned in full alert lessened his bravado, so he decided that he was no longer interested in feudal engagements.

Just then a drop of cave water dripped from a stalactite and landed on Vladimir's nose, and he became seized by a profusion of nerves. He barked anxiously as he ran back up the staircase, "Let's get out of here!"

He grabbed Laquita's hand and they swiftly scuttered up the final steps while practically climbing over each other's heads, and thrust open the storm shelter doors, finally scrambling out into the freedom of fresh, unfettered air.

CHAPTER 10

The doyen Walking Ghost Tour guide was in the midst of delivering his oration describing the haunted nature of the Old City Jail of Port City, South Carolina. He was sharing the most popular story in his prodigious repertoire, that on the night of every full moon, from the third story of the spiral staircase, the ghost of Ella Fitzgerald could be heard singing George Gershwin's soulful tune of "Summertime" from the opera Porgy and Bess, that had been composed only a few miles from the grounds of the civil war prison.

A fascinated, gullible tourist asked, "Does Ella have a backup trio accompanying her, or is she singing acapella?"

Precisely at that moment, the misplaced twosome emerged from the storm shelter, and scuffled onto the manicured grounds of the Old City Jail. They were not aware of their unkempt appearance as they began to brush themselves off. Vladimir's shirt was unbuttoned and untucked and his belt was hanging loose. Laquita's hair was disheveled, and one of her shoes that had fallen off was in her hand. Both of their faces were streaked with mud, and they were both covered head to toe in a dusting of white powder that had filled the air due to the clandestine pill distribution center. In the rays of the setting sun, the Walking Ghost Tour audience thought that they were seeing zombies and assumed that this was part of the paid entertainment. The tourists all tittered at the divertissement, offered enthusiastic applause, and began taking photos, asking permission to pose for selfies with them.

As they posed for the cameras against the backdrop of the Old City Jail, The Walking Ghost Tour guide observed the fire from across the Local Main Avenue and commented, "The smoke is getting really thick from that fire. Are they ever going to put out that blaze?"

Vladimir and Laquita asked, "What fire? Speaking of fire, let's get back to the Deli before Mr. Olive fires us both!"

The game of Seven Card Stud was in full swing, and Mahogany was already playing the Gigue, the last movement of the Bach Suite. He had become oblivious to his surroundings, engrossed in the Baroque music, striving to combine his expressive phrasing with the technical prowess on the viola that he practiced hours each day to perfect.

Meanwhile, Vladimir and Laquita entered through the back door of the Local Greek Deli and disappeared into the restroom for a spell in order to appear passably tidied up. Laquita noticed that the sticky substance on her hand was colorless, similar to tree sap. "How bizarre," she commented, unable to peg what it could be, but relieved that it was not blood.

The two then emerged into the dining room of the Local Greek Deli and tried to remain inconspicuous as they resumed their duties. They slowed their gait upon entering the empty dining room and saw the abandoned food and unused styrofoam boxes on all the tables. They were not yet aware of the fire across the street and scratched their heads in puzzlement as they looked around the room. The only thing in its normal place was the poker players at Table 16 and Mahogany, all seemingly oblivious to the absence of the Monday Night Regulars.

Laquita then saw her parental unit sitting at Table 16, and at once she became adrenalized. She reviewed in her mind her plot to blackmail and humiliate him. Seeing The Fifth sitting there, smug in his pin-stripe Tilby hat, and double-breasted suit, looking like the photo on his blog where the caption underneath it read, "Make America White Again," totally incensed her. "He is such a despicable schmuck," she thought, becoming even more motivated to carry on with her plans to blight his career as well as his reputation.

Vladimir waited for the final cadence of Mahogany's solo Bach Suite, and sat in his special musician chair. He put his foot on the collapsible footrest, placed his elbow on his knee, and adroitly tuned the strings on his guitar. Maestro Ding then leaned over, and in a voice quite pretentious yet nevertheless friendly, requested, "Could you boys please play a Puccini aria for me?"

The two musicians gave each other a look, but agreed, and flipped through the pages of their "Music for Two" gig books. They began to perform a duet version of "O Mio Babbino Caro," which made the symphony conductor smile in approval as he relaxed back in his chair.

Maestro Ding was reminiscing about times past that no one in his captive audience believed, but, as all seasoned poker players tend to do, they skillfully masked their dubiety as he continued to bloviate.

"When I was Leonard Bernstein's assistant conductor at the New York Philharmonic, when I was only 18 years old, he told me that I was his most favored and dearest disciple. I tried not to brag to the other assistant conductors before me, but what could I do?" he asked rhetorically in feigned humbleness.

"I knew from the time I was young that we were destined to work together. I knew that we had a special bond, a special love."

Mahogany heard this through the strains of Puccini and rolled his eyes over his viola at Vladimir.

"Once, I shared with the great Master a video of me conducting my orchestra in Germany, the Staatsorchester of Hamburg, where I am the life-time tenured Music Director and Artistic Director and Principal Conductor. I was leading my orchestra in a performance of Bernstein's composition 'Symphonic Dances from West Side Story.' Lenny gasped when he saw me on the video. He was so moved that he could not keep back his tears. He embraced me, kissed my forehead, and told me that I must be his spiritual soul mate." The symphony Maestro swooned with ill-concealed braggadocio as he re-enacted his memories with dramatic flailing arms.

The Fifth could not bridle his repugnance at the soliloquy and took a jab at his poker colleague. "Tell me, boy, are all of y'all Chinks this completely gay, or is it that fru fru music y'all conduct that changes all y'all into yellow-bellied pantywaists? And what kind of illegal immigrant name is Ding, anyway? What is y'all's first name? James? James Ding?" He let out a chortle.

The Maestro inhaled slowly and deeply and remained silent for a moment stroking his purple beret. He was accustomed to States Rights' outbursts of racist slurs and refused to take the bait. Instead he calmly responded, "In China, we state our names in reverse order than you do in America. Our last name is first, and our first name is last..."

The Fifth couldn't resist interrupting to say, "That figures, all y'all slant eyes are so backwards, y'all can't even say y'all's names in the right order. So, then, again, tell us, what is y'all's first name?"

Maestro Ding placed two cards on the table, saying, "I'll take two, please." Then he continued, "My first name is Dong, which means 'winter' in Chinese. My mother said that a fresh snow had just fallen before she gave birth to me, and that the silence was beautiful. She says because of me, winter is her favorite season."

"Dong? You're serious. So y'all's full name is Dong Ding?" asked the Fifth with a smirk on his face.

"No, in correct Chinese order, my full name is Ding Dong."

Mr. Olive had been lost in his own thoughts throughout this colloquy. Wondering if he would be forced to evacuate when Hurricane Camille made landfall at week's end. How would he pay off that ruthless judge his debt from Señora Conche's court winning, with his business shut down for days? He worried as he calculated the impact of the impending storm. But upon hearing that his friend's name was Ding Dong, he could not stifle his laughter.

As soon as Nazoon released his guffaws, Dr. Gamble let loose, and the game was temporarily stalled while peals of laughter reverberated through the air.

"Ding Dong! Ha ha! Omg! That's hysterical!"

"Ding Dong... Ding Dong... Who's there?"

"Is he crazy? No, he's just a Ding Dong! Ha ha ha ha!!!"

Someone dropped their cards face up, but no one minded. After the laughter died down, and tears were wiped from their eyes, The Constitution was consulted for procedural due process to be followed when cards were accidentally revealed.

Laquita approached Table 16 to take orders for food and drink. The Fifth was waiting for his fresh cards to be dealt, and for the first time since his daughter started her undercover employment at the Local Greek Deli, he gave her a lengthy gander.

For a moment, Laquita feared he may recognize her as Jane Margaret, jeopardizing her plan to destroy him.

Instead, The Fifth remarked, "Say, Nazoon, y'all used to hire pretty white girls to work here. Now, I have to look at her ugly face?"

Mr. Olive coughed in surprise. He was accustomed to

outrageous evil-minded insults, but this one crossed the line. He had a mind to give The Fifth an unceremonious punt out the emergency exit door.   But right as the restaurateur was about to get out of his chair, and give the indecorous Esquire the boot, the business owner remembered how the bigoted attorney had acquired the Local Greek Deli a liquor license two years in a row in lieu of payment for one of his Monday night gambling debts.

And then Mr. Olive remembered when the ungentlemanly councilman changed a B rating from the Health Department for having his lettuce on display at 50 degrees, to an A rating before the low mark was put on public display.

Mr. Kalamatamidis caught himself mid motion, calculating that the presence of States Rights Gist favored the Local Greek Deli's bottom line, and so he sat back down, and remained mute.

"One of these days," thought Mr. Olive, fuming to himself. "One of these days, I'm really going to let this old geezer have it."

CHAPTER 11

Mr. FBI man shrugged his shoulders, and decided that apprehending the depraved and lubricious violinist, Ferdinand Lombardini, could wait another day. He figured that the creator of illicit videos featuring young children was guaranteed an unfavorable future in prison in due course, and he was famished, so he dropped his search, and headed next door to the Local Greek Deli for a large lamb gyro sandwich with extra tzatziki sauce. By now, the police were directing traffic to make room for the fire trucks and emergency vehicles on the Local Main Avenue.

The federal operative was waiting his turn for the police officer to allow him to drive through the intersection. Just then, a phone call from his superior changed his ambitions of nursing a scotch on the rocks later that evening while watching reruns of American Ninja Warrior.

"Agent Jones, you have another assignment. You are the one closest to the vicinity, so you start the investigation to determine who started the fire at the Shack of Sit. Start looking around to see who looks suspicious. We all know how arsonists love to watch their own fires."

Agent Jones hung up the phone and heaved a heavy sigh of disappointment. "Arson cases are always the most excruciating," he reflected, "because oftentimes, it is a decorated firefighter that turns out to be the culprit." He sighed a second time as he pulled into the parking lot of the Local Greek Deli.

MarvLee and Conner were sitting in the congested traffic, the car gear in neutral, the father fuming about what he had just seen on those tapes, and the son excited to see dozens of flashing blue and red lights and men in uniform. As he brought his attention back to the present moment, MarvLee realized that the fire was increasing steadily in size, and certainly the Fire Chief was calling for all hands on deck. With that thought, he turned into the parking lot behind the Local Greek Deli.

"Conner, you be a good boy, and sit in this deli to eat yo' dinner while I go help fight this fire, Yo momma should be inside cause she be working Mondays, you good?" MarvLee instructed as he adoringly stroked his son's head and handed him some cash.

He choked back emotion as he gazed at his darling boy, feeling queasy from the betrayal at how his deceitful friend, Ferdinand, had taken advantage of his precious child all these years.

"I'll deal with dat good-for-nuttin scoundrel soon enough," MarvLee thought to himself.

Conner was overjoyed that he and his mother could both together watch his Local Hero father in action from the Local Greek Deli's windows, and scampered out of the car enthusiastically, skipping into the restaurant.

MarvLee opened the trunk of his car to retrieve his spare uniform that he always kept on hand. Tears of rage began to well up as he pushed aside the large black duffle bag filled with videos in order to reach for his helmet. He began walking toward the Shack of Sit with the duffle bag of videos flung over his shoulder with the intent to throw the knapsack filled with turpitude into the fire, and make sure that the incriminating evidence turned to smoke.

But just as he was stepping away from his car, and placing his helmet on his head, the surly FBI agent was closing the driver's door of his car on the opposite side of the parking lot of the Local Greek Deli. The operative spotted MarvLee with the fireman's helmet on and gave him a suspicious eye.

Anyone in fire gear was a potential suspect as the arsonist, and Agent Jones already had doubts about the rectitude of this chap after meandering with him through the Tillman Auditorium a short while earlier. But he decided to leave him well enough alone until after he had dined on his large lamb gyro sandwich with extra tzatziki sauce at the Local Greek Deli.

MarvLee saw the look of suspicion from the operative and began to fret as he realized that he had just been spotted holding the black duffle bag filled with the nasty videos. What if Mr. FBI man suspected that he was an accomplice to Ferdinand? That would explain his suspicious glance.

"Oh no, Ferdinand, you conniving good-for-nuttin low-life. I aint be lettin you get me mixed up in your sins. No way be any o dat goin on here. No, siree," he thought to himself as he nervously looked around, trying to figure out what to do.

He noticed that the door to the storage shed of the Local Greek Deli was slightly open. "I'll put the videos in here until Mr. FBI man leaves, then I'll throw them in the fire," MarvLee plotted as he hastily tossed the black duffle bag into the granite storage shed, landing it behind the top-loading freezer filled to the brim with Greek-style boneless, skinless chicken. He then ran across the street, putting on the rest of his fire gear as he went.

As MarvLee approached the inferno, he was overcome with foreboding. He felt compelled to send Nonna a text message in case misfortunes were to fall upon him. "Chucho's bag be in Greek Deli storage out back." He pushed the send icon, put his phone on a parked fire truck, then he ran to Fire Chief McGee and informed him, "Reporting for duty, sir!"

Grateful for another man, the Chief instructed, "Yes, yes, I need more men inside! All of you, get any hose you can!" as he waved his arm at the dozen volunteer firemen that had descended onto the scene garbed in everything from full gear to shorts and t-shirts, as they had all dropped everything they were doing to come assist.

In the pandemonium that ensued, Fire Chief McGee lost track of how many men were in the building. A police officer ran to him and said, "Chief, the owner, Mr. Marion, is trapped inside. He's in the back office."

The Chief tried to remain calm as he ordered more men to get their axes and chop a hole in the wall to get the business owner out. At this point, the Shack of Sit was being assailed by its own ammunition. The hope that the fire might burn itself out proved a vain one as masonry was sailing in crazy abandon. The Battalion Chief and the two senior firemen had travelled to the center of the main room by picking their way just like mountain climbers through the furniture. The firemen at the back entrance axed furiously at the locked door, and when opened, it sucked in oxygen, sending hissing clouds of thick piney smoke into the firmament. This afforded only partial relief, and the determined flames kept blazing away.

Men continued to enter the building with hoses big and small, maintaining laser focus to extinguish the stubborn flames as they licked toward more fuel-producing furniture. Chief McGee ordered the team of Ladder 5 to enter from the highest windows and tackle the flames from above. It was a risky mission that the men did not relish, but they did so with righteous duty.

MarvLee embarked on a punitive expedition into the inferno, hoping to find, and then help his friend that had traded shifts with him for that fateful Monday summer night at Port City, South Carolina. He entered the main showroom that was still dark as night. But with his helmet light, he was able to recognize the reflective sticker of the volunteer squad's logo on his friend's helmet. He was on the floor, trapped under a pile of burning recliner chairs. He rushed to help him.

Only moments later, the structure began to make menacing noises that all the firemen recognized as direful and lived in constant dread of hearing. At the same time, the Battalion Chief began continuously pulling his safety life-line, communicating the signal for extreme distress.

The senior fireman inside the building with the Battalion Chief called over the radio with the word no one ever longs to hear, "Mayday! Mayday!"

A few seconds later, the radio speaker transmitted a message of doom, "Car One, please tell my wife 'I love you'" followed by snippets of the Lord's Prayer. "In Jesus' name. Amen."

With that, the roof's beam of the truss collapsed onto the labyrinth of furniture below trapping an undetermined number of firefighters under its enormous expanse of hot molten steel. Chief McGee's equable nature became unhinged as he frantically tried to determine how many men were in the building. As he was forcing his eyes to focus at the roster, a volunteer tugged at his arm crying out, "Look, Chief!"

The Chief looked up to see the smoke had transformed into the texture of thick cotton candy, an ominous sign. "Everybody out! Everyone evacuate! Evacuate now! Get out now. Get the hell out now!" he shouted hysterically over the radio.

The blaze was in no mood to wait. And within seconds it cast a pall over an already solemn event. The entire showroom exploded at once, producing a conflagration of historic proportions.

The Local TV camera crews were ecstatic with the dramatic footage, until they realized that it was immediately evident that anyone who was remaining inside would no longer have the occasion of inhaling another breath. With unspoken agreement and understanding, the cameramen eyed one another from their various vantage points, and in unison, they all bowed their heads, folded their hands in prayer, and stopped filming the tragedy for a few moments in respectful civility.

Like fire ants being hosed out of their dirt mound, scores of firemen were hurriedly scattering out of the building in all directions. Those fortunate to have made it out in time were bearing the wounds of battle, with thumbs dangling, skin missing, third degree burns, and scorched lungs.

The Fire Chief Monte McGee was now put in the most unenviable, soul-wrenching predicament, in which he had to immediately send yet even more men into harm's way. The inferno was an impatient enemy and did not allow him time to digest emotions at leisure. The next several hours forced the Chief to give commands quickly, and on their results would hang issues momentous enough to chill the blood.

Laquita and Conner had been watching the fire from Table 13 at the Local Greek Deli. They watched through the blue and yellow curtains as MarvLee entered the Shack of Sit, and they held their breath, anxiously waiting to see him exit the building. They waited some more.

"I'm sure your father left from the back door of the building, and we just didn't see him, Sweetie," Laquita said in an unconvincing attempt to calm her son's anxiety as she stroked his head.

Soon after the blast, the Local Police of Port City, South Carolina, commanded everyone in the vicinity to evacuate. The Monday Night Regulars slowly drifted back to the Local Greek Deli to gather their belongings, shaken into murmuring and whispering among themselves about the awfulness of the ongoing catastrophe.

Mr. Olive consulted The Constitution and declared that the explosion at the Shack of Sit qualified as a "force majeure" and therefore the game could be stopped immediately, and all debts erased. He required that all the Monday Night Regulars pay for their meals before they left, whether they had eaten them or not. Also, he ascertained that King, Laquita, and Ernest had cleansed all surfaces. Hurriedly, he grabbed his walking stick and escorted his poker friends to their cars. Then he waited patiently for his musicians to pack up their gig bags and offered them each a beer to take home with them.

Finally, the Local Greek Deli was empty. Mr. Olive went to the bakery to collect his wallet and keys, but, first, he sat down, took off his fisherman's cap, and ran his fingers through his salt and pepper hair. Only then, when all was dark and quiet at the restaurant, and he was sitting alone looking at the photo of his darling Zorika, running his worry beads through his left hand, did the reality of the severity of Mr. Marion's plight dawn on him.

"My God, he may lose everything. He might even lose his life," he realized, surprising even himself with the unfamiliar feeling of compassion that unexpectedly arose from his heart. He even made himself squirm as he considered dismissing his original intention of taking Mr. Marion to court if the fire negatively affected his restaurant sales.

CHAPTER 12

Concertmaster violinist Ferdinand Lombardini was sick with chagrin that the skeletons in his closet that had been successfully concealed for an impressively long stretch were now being unceremoniously exposed. He knew straight away that the FBI had not one whit of solicitude for Chucho, the waterpipe. He was no fool and knew that the authorities had bigger fish to fry than catching grass smokers. As incriminating as the VHS videos of little Amber and Conner assuredly were, Ferdinand had confidence that a good defense attorney, someone like the Local City Councilman, the Honorable Councilor States Rights Gist, V Esquire, could deftly argue a preposterous exoneration on his behalf.

But what would undoubtedly rocket the violinist into an imbroglio was the material contained in his laptop computer. That's why he grabbed his silver 15-inch MacBook with backlit retina display that was hidden underneath the chips in the cedar chest at the back of the music room. He had to devise a plan to dispose of it fast. As he ran out of his house, with the crime laden computer under his arm, he slowed his pace to gawk at the colossal fire at the Shack of Sit whose property adjoined his back yard.

Giving himself no time to ponder the consequences, he rushed to the green metal dumpster behind the furniture store that was hosting its own bonfire, and flung the laptop over the edge, and into the flames. He was feeling shamefaced, even to himself, that he was mournful to lose so many years of collected nefarious footage.

He watched the dumpster, oblivious to the chaos that bearded him, self-absorbed in grieving the loss of his fetish documentation. As soon as he determined that the MacBook must surely be melting, he noticed the bedlam that he had entered, and was horrified to see several firemen, some of whom were not even in uniform, furiously struggling to rescue Mr. Marion from his office where he had been trapped under a burning fallen beam and was choking on toxic smoke.

Ferdinand and Mr. Marion had been neighbors for over a decade and had become boon companions. When Ferdinand saw the severity of Mr. Marion's injuries as he was being extricated through the axed hole in the wall, the graveness of the situation finally hit him. Most certainly, he was in a conundrum, but his good friend looked as if he might expire at any moment. He rushed up to his wounded ally and offered to accompany him in the ambulance as it raced off to the hospital.

Once at the Emergency Room, the doctors, nurses, x-ray technicians, burn specialists, and anesthesiologist all descended upon the furniture store owner in a flurry of controlled mayhem, and within moments determined that the ceiling beam had landed on Mr. Marion's kidneys, and crushed both into wads of useless tissue. Someone rushed out of the whirlwind of activity, and informed Ferdinand that his compadre would need a kidney transplant immediately.

Ferdinand, without batting an eye, said, "He can have one of mine!"

The molester of unsuspecting youngsters did not have to offer twice. The ER nurse immediately stabbed his arm to determine his blood type, and before he could have second thoughts or voice a protest, the burly nurse's aides threw Ferdinand onto a gurney, knocked him out with a gas mask, and began preparing the virtuoso violinist to immolate an auxiliary organ for his pal, Mr. Marion.

CHAPTER 13

Mahogany felt uneasy leaving for home, but the police insisted that everyone evacuate. Somehow, as he looked at the Shack of Sit's volcanic plume in his rearview mirror, he felt as if he were leaving his pet at the veterinarian to be put to sleep without saying goodbye. When he walked into his apartment, to calm his nerves, he lit an incense stick next to the life-size statue of the goddess Saraswati, and began to chant an invocation, "Oh Goddess Saraswati, protect us from all forms of ignorance..."

After repeating several more verses of the ancient hymn, he knelt on both knees, and placed his forehead on the floor in reverence. He went to the kitchen, and opened the Mythos beer that Mr. Olive had offered him, sat on the recliner and invited his Maine Coon cat, Ludwig, onto his lap and began stroking his head, then scratching the itchy spot under his feline friend's furry chin. Soon, Mahogany drifted off to sleep while Ludwig sprawled out full length on his owner's legs and began purring at full volume.

As the moments of reverie turned into hours of slumber,

Mahogany's consciousness meandered into a deep dream state which escorted his awareness into a subtle realm where he came upon an esoteric scene. There was a large ring of fire on the blue ground. He saw a person lying motionless in the center. At first, he thought that he was watching the scene of Wotan's farewell to Brunhilde in Wagner's opera, "The Ring." But as he approached the ring of fire, he saw that the person in the center was MarvLee. The Local Hero volunteer firefighter turned toward Mahogany, his face was tranquil and peaceful. Mahogany felt a calming stillness indicating that everything was safe and secure. He noticed a supreme contentment in his heart.

The fire ring began to dissolve, and as it was disappearing, MarvLee said to Mahogany, "Destroy the bag in the shed. Do it for Conner."

Then all that remained was a velvety blackness. Then a beautiful woman appeared in a new ring of fire who looked like the goddess Saraswati. She was inviting Mahogany to join her in the fire. Her large brown eyes were kind, deep, and soulful.

He asked her, "How do I know I'll be safe? How do I know that the fire won't hurt me?"

He took her extended hand and joined her in the fire. He was floating on his back. His body melted into the fire, and he then found his entire being wafting in a sea of tranquil serenity.

Mahogany awoke early the next morning, forgetting his dream, but feeling its effects of peaceful repose. Ludwig had long since left his lap and was in his usual stakeout on the windowsill checking for avian activity. The Adjunct Professor of the Local Community College who was hired to teach Music Appreciation, but was also the Instructor of Viola, Double Bass, Music Theory, Ethnomusicology, Ear Training, and the History of Rock and Roll, felt different somehow. His forehead was tingling, and he had this inexplicable sensation of being in love. He sensed as if his heart had expanded beyond his physical body, and for no reason in particular he was smiling broadly.

He looked around, and all the objects in his apartment appeared to possess a coruscating luster. He was astonished at how everything he gazed upon was so beautifully opalescent. He viewed the scenery outside the window and beheld the sidewalk that laced the parking lot of the apartment building. Its effulgence was breathtaking. The cracks in the concrete mesmerized him. He looked at the empty wooden stand where his Double-bass used to recline before it was stolen out of his car while he was unloading groceries a week ago and gasped at the heavenliness of its craftsmanship. Had the world always been this iridescent and enthralling, and he was just now perceiving it?

He turned on the TV to see if there were any news about the fire. Just then his phone rang. He saw on the caller ID that the Dean of Instruction of the Local Community College, Mahogany's boss, was on the other end, and he had some news. He listened to his boss on the phone while he watched the press conference that was airing live on all the Local TV Stations.

CHAPTER 14

The rays of Tuesday morning's dawn had revealed a stark new reality for the Port City of South Carolina. A spare conductor's podium and music stand were borrowed from the Tillman auditorium and set up for the press conference to be held on the Local Main Avenue. The surroundings of the Shack of Sit were scarcely less than infernal. Original lineaments of the furniture warehouse were only dimly discernable, its ramparts were chopped and truncated, and its interior a waste of rubble. It was now a great rectangular windrow of loose tangled steel and debris, with wisps of smoke still issuing forth. It was an eerie reality one might experience in a nightmare.

The Mayor of the fine-spun populace of the Port City of South Carolina was a shade paler than usual as he stepped up to the microphone. His expression of consternation did not reveal the true depth of the anguish he felt inside. He cleared his throat, and quickly realized that he was too emotional to speak, so he handed the microphone to Fire Chief Monte McGee.

The Chief had not left the scene since he had arrived the night before, and it was evident from his haggard face what the grueling ordeal of the last twelve hours had had on him. He took off his helmet, and began to speak, to give the world the official report of the sorrowful, grim news. But as soon as he opened his mouth, he became shaken by sobs that gripped him for several moments before he regained his composure.

The TV news reporters respectfully maintained silence and waited patiently. A few of them became stricken with emotion and began to weep. The hum of the engine of the one remaining fire truck accompanied the poignant moment along with the chirps and songs of the morning coastal birds.

The reporters were given the names of the nine fallen firemen who perished in the Shack of Sit fire, in the order of rank. The Battalion Chief, the Lieutenant, the Captain, one, two, three names... the two Senior Firefighters, four, five names... the three Probationary Firefighters, six, seven, eight names, then the last name to be read, "And Volunteer Hero firefighter, MarvLee Borman..." the ninth name.

Fire Chief McGee could maintain his poise no longer and handed the microphone back to the Mayor as he choked uncontrollably on grief-stricken tears.

FBI Agent Jones had scrutinized every potential suspect during the long hours of the fire. He monitored every attendant at the press conference and waited patiently for someone to reveal the slightest flicker of guilty behavior, but saw none emitting from any spectator. No one had divulged the classic telltale signs of hero complex that would broadcast an arsonist to a questioning professional eye. There had been no females in the building feigning victim complex. His exhaustive background check on Mr. Marion revealed that he was the only owner of the building for fifteen years and had not overestimated its insurance value. He was well loved with no one harboring a grudge toward him nor any ex-wives plotting revenge.

But to finally rule out arson, Agent Jones now was focused on the point of origin of the fire. By morning, it was determined that the fire originally had ignited in the green metal dumpster behind the main showcase room, indicating an accidental combustion. The fire professionals had taken samples of ashes to the crime laboratory to determine the chemical makeup of the ignition and accelerant. Agent Jones was hopeful that soon both he and the world would know how the fire started.

Mr. Olive learned that the memorial service for the nine fallen firemen would be held on Friday morning next door to the Local Greek Deli in the Tillman Auditorium, and that thousands of mourners would be attending. He realized that a sizable percentage of those mourners would perchance come for lunch at the Local Greek Deli after the solemn event, but before the Mayor's voluntary evacuation order now in place for the approaching Hurricane Camille. As he calculated the positive monetary effect, his eyes became alive with enterprise.

Suddenly, he was no longer annoyed at his poker colleague, Mr. Marion, for taking away business due to customers being detoured by yellow police tape surrounding the entire city block. He decided to drop the idea of taking him to court as soon as he was released from the hospital, since now it was evident to the Greek businessman that he was able to make great capital out of the situation.

CHAPTER 15

The solemn summer Friday morning of Port City's nine fallen firemen's memorial service arrived, and Eli Goldsmith bumped his head on the wall of the underground tunnel, knocking off his yarmulke as he descended into the storm shelter on the far end of the manicured lawn of the Old City Jail. The revered cantor of the Local Synagogue that boasted of being the oldest Jewish congregation this side of the Atlantic Ocean was addressed by the genteel men and women of Port City, South Carolina, as the Learned Mr. Moreh Eli. And though the public man assumed that principled behavior was his norm, for he was a compact man with inbred Southern courtesy; in fact, the honored holy man possessed an exterior polish which concealed a dark strain of violence under the skin.

The blue skies that were being rudely invaded by the outer cloud rings of approaching Hurricane Camille were witnessing the entire community attending the memorial service at Tillman Auditorium. So no one noticed the pious peddler stealthily entering the wooden doors of the storm shelter, and heading to the bottom of the staircase in the cavern with stalactites and stalagmites that led to the distribution center of illicit prescription pills.

The Learned Mr. Moreh Eli was rubbing the leather kippah hat on his thigh to remove the slime it collected from the wall when he noticed that his flashlight was missing from the small table. Eli had left the flashlight illuminated last Sabbath when he exited the secret cavern after sundown. He had lost track of time and did not leave the cave until dark. And according to the 39 Melachot of Shabbat, he was not allowed to extinguish light, so he had left it sitting on the table in the small room.

Now, this eventful summer Friday morning in June, he had to plan ahead. There was Hurricane Camille due to arrive at sundown later that day. The mammoth Category 4 storm, headed for a direct hit on the Southern port city had begun to rain on the mourning town.

Eli was determined to keep his merchandise from becoming ruined in the flood-prone cave, so he began to remove the mountains of white pill packs from the Tupperware bins, and thrust them into his mountain-climber, black canvas duffle backpack to take them to his house. He pondered what to do given that it was risky to carry the bag out of the cavern during daylight and the rain. But he could not wait until it was dark, because also, according to the 39 Melachot of Sabbath, after sundown, he was not permitted carry anything.

Normally on Fridays, as part of his duty as cantor, the devout man led the weekly *Shalom Aleichem* song with his exquisite singing voice. But this Friday happened to be Rosh Chodesh Tamuz, and so he also had to plan on beginning his fast. His day was very full, which required that he strategize carefully. He considered all the options and elected to stash the merchandise in the Local Greek Deli's storage shed instead, rather than his home.

So he dragged the black canvas, mountain backpack through the slimy underground tunnel toward the Greek Deli's storage shed, and climbed the short ladder underneath the trap door that he had discovered years earlier. He pulled down the trap door and heaved the illicit drugs up through the opening and into the storage shed's floor. He pulled himself through the opening and, with his foot, pushed the black pack behind the top-loading freezer filled with boneless, skinless chicken.

As he stood in the dark and stifling heat of the storage shed, he opted to return to the cavern to retrieve the Anschutz 1781 rifle. Making sure the trigger was locked, he slid the stolen firearm into the storage shed, and pulled the trap door closed. Satisfied that his goods were safe until after Sabbath and passage of Hurricane Camille, the Learned Mr. Moreh, Eli Goldsmith, snuck back through the clandestine tunnel, and climbed the steps leading to the storm shelter doors that opened up to the Old City Jail's well-manicured grounds. Repositioning his yarmulke and brushing himself off, the unscrupulous cantor determined that he had not been detected, and casually joined the crowd entering the Tillman Auditorium the next block over to attend the firemen's memorial service.

CHAPTER 16

The team of doctors at the Local Medical University was satisfied that Mr. Marion would not reject the kidney he had received from his buddy, Ferdinand Lombardini, but neither one of the fellows would be permitted to leave the Intensive Care Unit anytime in the foreseeable future. Nonna had sent her grandchildren to a friend's house and had spent the last few days checking in on her son. Ferdinand had several complications from the surgery and remained unconscious. As Nonna observed him through the window, even though she admired his generosity in donating one of his internal organs instantly, without the slightest vacillation in his decision, she was conflicted in her emotions, now that she knew the contents of those nasty VHS videos of Amber and Conner that had been hiding right under her nose for years ever since she moved in with him after his wife died.

She stood at the window of the ICU, watching Ferdinand's breathing, hearing the beeps and whirring of the monitors connected to every orifice of his body. She was a prudent woman and ascertained that remaining loyal to a child molester currently being pursued by the FBI, no matter how one construed it, was a categorical path to a life of misery. She shuddered to think of the possibility that her two grandsons were featured on any of the videos and hoped that MarvLee had destroyed them already so that no one would have to find out.

Just then a text message came through on her phone. It was from MarvLee: "Chucho's bag be in Greek Deli storage out back."

"Hmm, that's a strange message. I wonder why it appeared on my phone just today, and not when he sent it before he died?" she wondered, but decided to ignore it. Instead, Nonna contemplated the vital respiratory tube that connected to her squalid son's oxygen supply. "How simple it would be to accidentally disconnect that tube," she thought.

As she considered the outcome, knowing that a flood of good wishes would come her way as everyone regarded Ferdinand as a hero organ donor rather than a dishonorable pervert, the idea became more appealing. As she further contemplated the sizeable life insurance policy payout, Nonna Lombardini's eyes became alive with enterprise.

"What other choices do I really have?" she asked herself.

She began to scrutinize the juncture where the oxygen tube connected to the supply tank and calculate the number of seconds and force required to snap it off. Determinedly, she reached for the door to the ICU ward, intent on following through with the evil action, when suddenly a hand landed on her shoulder.

Dr. Gamble had just finished his seven hundredth operation of the year in the transgender surgery department, securing funds for a trip with his wife to the Fiji Islands, when he decided to check in on Ferdinand and Nonna at the ICU. He had known the Lombardini family for many years and came by to see if he could offer a sympathetic ear. Nonna loved Dr. Gamble, despite his embarrassing habit of bellowing out personal information in public places.

As he stood there, gazing at Ferdinand through the window,

she remembered how the loud transgender surgeon passed by her in the waiting room of the image specialist x-ray center a few years ago, after she had surgery to remove a kidney stone. In the waiting room teaming with other patients, he boomed out good-naturedly, "Nonna, you don't look too bad given that you just had your urethra sliced into pieces to get that enormous thing out. Have you passed gas yet? Now remember, drink plenty of fluids. Your pee needs to be the color of water, y'all hear?"

Nonna shook her head as she recalled the cringe-worthy moment. Just then she remembered the text from MarvLee and realized that the nasty videos had not been destroyed. Being quick on her feet, she entreated Dr. Gamble, "Say, Dr. Gamble, I have a favor to ask of you, if it's no trouble for you, of course."

"Name it, my dear friend. I will do thy bidding. What is it?" he assured her.

"MarvLee had intended to bring me an overnight bag, a black canvas duffle bag, so that I could sleep at the hospital. But when he was called in to help fight the fire at the Shack of Sit, he texted me that he left the bag in the storage shed back of Mr. Olive's Deli. I completely forgot about it until now. Can you fetch that bag for me? I would appreciate it very much."

Dr. Gamble was delighted that he could help his friend and agreed without hesitation. Immediately, he caught the next elevator and headed to the Local Greek Deli's mountain granite storage shed to retrieve the black canvas duffle bag.

As soon as Nonna saw the elevator button illuminate that the ground floor had been reached, she looked around the nurses' station. Two of them were gossiping while pretending to study charts. A phlebotomist strolled by, wheeling a cart loaded with tubes of patients' blood. A burn specialist doctor was examining Mr. Marion down the hall, when suddenly a flurry of activity ensued.

"Incoming injured. Several casualties. Tour boat capsized due to high ocean waves from approaching Hurricane Camille. All personnel report immediately," Nonna heard over the hospital sound system.

As she watched the medical employees of the Local Medical University rush toward the incoming injured, and away from her son, Ferdinand, the pragmatic mother of a pedophile under FBI investigation recognized the opportunity and seized the moment. Without a single flinch, Nonna opened the door to her offspring's ICU quarters, approached his bed, and deftly removed the tube to his oxygen supply. And for good measure, she grabbed a syringe filled with ibuprofen, harmless to the healthy, but deadly to a kidney donor, and stabbed the needle into his saline solution bag, leading the fatal dose of nsaids directly into the veins of her smirched and seedy descendant.

Agent Jones quickly pulled his head back around the corner of the nurses' station, so as not to be spotted by the murderous Lombardini matriarch. Unknown to the vengeful mother of the soon-to-be-dead concertmaster of the Local Symphony Orchestra, he had been spying on her for the last hour and witnessed the entire event.

Scratching his head at this unexpected moment, he empathized. "An ethical quandary, I must admit," thought the FBI man. "I can't say I wouldn't do the same thing myself if I were in her predicament. I suppose I could say I was distracted by the incoming injured boat tourists and didn't see anything," he pondered.

CHAPTER 17

The entire expansive parking lot of the Tillman Auditorium and all the lanes of the Local Main Avenue were besieged by a snarl of cars which volunteer liveried traffic controllers were trying to untangle with hopelessly uncoordinated signals and gesticulations. Eventually, by an unseen magical force that could not be explained by any witness, order suddenly descended, and a wide path was formed, like the parting of the Red Sea, to make way for the majestic military escort which had begun marching in splendid array from the fire station four blocks away toward the auditorium accompanying the pallbearers for all nine caskets. Stirring notes of the marching brass band's stoic fanfare alerted the multitudes that the memorial service was about to commence.

The musicians of the Local Symphony Orchestra had consulted their union contract with the Local Chapter of the Musician's National Federation and concluded that they were not in violation of labor rules if they volunteered to perform at the memorial service. So as the pallbearers and military companies, led by the Local Policeman Color Guard, were entering the building and filing down the center aisle of the audience, and onto the main stage, the orchestra performed under the baton of Maestro Ding a soulful rendition of Purcell's 17th century aria "When I am Laid in Earth," while the lyrics were sung by a Local Soprano from the Local College.

"*When I am laid in earth, may my wrongs create no trouble in thy breast. Remember me, but ahh, forget my fate,*" entreated the singer with sorrowful tones, sustaining her plea for several moments until her voice faded into silence and the Maestro dropped his hands to his side as the orchestra musicians froze in position holding their instruments in place.

This was the cue for the Color Guard, with their white cotton gloves, to inaudibly lift their rifles into formation and begin their ceremonial offering. In that precise moment of stillness, a pack of Marlboro cigarettes fell out of the shirt pocket of the orchestra's perpetually drunken Russian clarinetist. The easily recognizable red and white cardboard box rolled noisily and conspicuously to the edge of the stage, to the mortification of his colleagues.

The memorial service had blossomed into a large affair over the course of the few days since the furniture store fire. After the Color Guard finished their ritual and stoically marched in the hushed atmosphere of the solemn event to the back of the auditorium, in perfect coordinated form and rhythm, creating a tenor of reverence and honor, several citizens of Port City, South Carolina, then shared stories of the fallen, gave speeches, and presented tableaux.

The service was to be climaxed with an address by the Mayor. But the careworn Mayor with his pouch-eyed expression had spoken only a few sentences when he made the grave error of looking out past the nine caskets and into the audience. The front five rows of the Tillman Auditorium were reserved for the families of the fallen, the injured firemen who were not hospitalized, and their families. As soon as he saw the widows and children crying and weeping, with nine caskets covered in the American flag, he became speechless. It was clear that he would not be able to utter another sound.

Local City Councilman, States Rights Gist V, recognized the moment as a highly prized political plum. He leapt to the stage and relieved the Mayor of his burden by taking over the podium. The audience was taken aback. Most of them were aware that States Rights had been elected despite the sulfurous vilification he made of anyone who opposed him. Some even regarded The Fifth as the very essence of evil. But despite the possible negative repercussions, he could not resist being in the vortex of any potential political turmoil.

The Fifth knew that many of his fans and readers of *The Herald* were assuredly sprinkled in among the thousands of spectators present and watching, and to those people, those easily excited fire-eating Palmetto men and other unassimilated Southerners, he began to pontificate. Fortified with potations that he carried in his ever-present flask, he began an improvisatory speech that covered his favorite topics of white supremacy, federal government conspiracies, and gun rights.

The Fifth was in excellent wind and held on for nearly an hour before it became evident that he was receiving a massive unanimity of disapproval from the audience. The Mayor regained his composure and approached States Rights on the stage, fixing him with a steely eye. The disgraceful councilman was unceremoniously booted off the podium by two security guards, at which point the Mayor of Port City resumed his speech where he had left off.

The memorial service reached its apogee when to the surprise, but heartfelt gratitude of the spectators, the famous opera star Tessie Borman rose from her seat. She donned a magnificent black gown with a patent leather bustier with sculptural shoulders, fingerless gloves up past the elbows, and a large floppy hat adorned with a 22 karat filigree veil that delicately covered her face. And with a ten-foot-long, gold-edged, black lace chiffon veil trailing behind her, she gracefully ascended the steps to the lip of the stage, stood herself nobly, and nodded at the Maestro.

Maestro Ding cued the symphony to play the rousing opening chords, to which the oldest sister of the fallen Local Volunteer Hero, MarvLee Borman, began to sing the patriotic strains of Irving Berlin's "God Bless America."

So moved were the people by her expressive, melodious cri de cœur, resonating from deep within her bosom, that the entire crowd stood to their feet simultaneously, swooning with tears in their eyes after her every utterance. Upon hitting the final high note of "*God bless America, my home sweet home….*" with full operatic voice that reverberated in the hearts of everyone as far away as the sands of the Atlantic beach, accompanied by the forces of the symphony orchestra's kettledrums and brass, a thunderous ovation continued for several minutes.

Thereafter, the roused emotion of the multitudes was directed at the nine caskets being escorted out of the Tillman Auditorium, followed by thirty pipers recruited from the Local Citadel Military School, playing "Amazing Grace" on the distinctive, poignant and piercing cries of their bagpipes.

Chapter 18

Ernest was grating a 28-pound block of feta cheese packed in brine as he gazed out the kitchen window of the Local Greek Deli. The overcast sky was drizzling the first deceptively light rains of Hurricane Camille that were soon to become buckets of flood waters in due course. Back at his native Pacific Island in Micronesia, the young chef had experienced his share of typhoons inundating the entire landscape with mudslides and tsunami waves, so he knew that a direct hit from a Category 4 storm heeded respect.

Earlier that morning, he had texted his many local relatives who lived in the Southern Palmetto state including his various cousins, who weren't actually his cousins. His aunts, uncles, nieces, nephews - none of whom were of any genuine blood relation. And his three sets of parents, whom no one seemed to know which ones actually conceived him. He warned them all that this afternoon would be a good time to pack up, and get ready to evacuate Port City, South Carolina.

This week's tub of feta cheese was a wet batch, annoying Ernest with the soggy crumbles that were normally dry and held their shape. He was wiping a splotch of feta that was stuck to his hand when he spotted the Regular Monday Night poker player, Dr. Gamble, through the window, entering the storage shed in the back parking lot, carrying himself as if he were on a mission.

The Local Transgender Surgeon gave only a cursory glance at the contents of the shed, and quickly grabbed the overnight black duffle bag that Nonna had requested that he fetch on her behalf. He was a bit startled to see the Anschutz 1781 rifle on the floor, but shrugged it off, assuming that Mr. Olive's eccentric personality inspired him to purchase it. Dr. Gamble placed the black duffle bag on the passenger seat, and as he pulled out of the parking lot, he realized that a bit more patience was in order since the traffic from the memorial service was still highly congested.

As he sat with the turn signal clicking rhythmically, waiting for a polite Southern, Port City resident to slow down, give a genteel wave of the hand, and let him make a left turn, he noticed that the bag sitting shotgun next to him was not completely closed. His inquisitive nature could not resist taking a gander. He raised his eyebrows when he pulled the zipper loose and espied enough oxycodone pills to cure the aches and pains of the entire population of the state of South Carolina for a month.

"Ah, clever lady," conjectured Dr. Gamble. "This must be Nonna's way of inviting me into her supplementary business for her retirement. She probably needed someone like me to assist her, while her son is out of commission in the hospital."

As the loud and embarrassing doctor calculated how many trips to Europe he could earn for himself and his wife by selling the illicit pills to his surgical patients, his eyes became alive with enterprise. Why, he could even use these pills to pay off some of his pesky gambling debts from the Monday night poker games at the Local Greek Deli. Then in true Southern form, a car slowed down, and its driver waved courteously to allow the doctor to make a left turn. The financially inspired surgeon, who presumed that he had been adroitly recruited into a clandestine income stream, headed back to the Local Medical University in order to give a wink, a nudge, and a handshake to Nonna Lombardini.

Meanwhile, Mr. Olive was enjoying working at his cash register as droves of Port City mourners decided to order carryout lunches of gyro sandwiches from the Local Greek Deli to eat while travelling the evacuation route to escape Hurricane Camille. Before too long, the supply of boneless skinless chicken diminished, so the businessman headed out to the top-loading freezer inside the granite storage shed.

Ernest had packaged and stored the grated feta cheese, and was now lightly brushing olive oil onto innumerable layers of paper-thin filo dough for a scrumptious batch of spanakopita, when he watched his boss Mr. Kalamatamidas III through the kitchen window place his myrtle wood walking stick against the door hinge, so as not to get trapped inside. Mr. Olive was so consumed with his mental calculations of the day's sales, that he did not notice the disheveled state of the shed, nor even the Anschutz 1781 rifle lying on the floor.

He lifted the door to the freezer and began filling his arms with frozen chicken. As he was closing the lid, his unbalanced gait made his knee bump into a black duffle bag with a VHS video sticking out.

"That's unusual. Maybe that belongs to Ernest," thought Mr. Olive absentmindedly.

Just then a video fell out of the bag and landed by the door next to his walking stick. The proud Persian Greek would not have given it any mind except he noticed that the label on the video cover said "Zora: Lesson 6."

He immediately dropped the frozen chicken and stooped

down to grab the video. As he snapped opened the vinyl cover, a photograph with a disturbing image that had been tucked under the video cassette fell to the floor. Grandfather Ya Ya's hands began to tremble as he reached down and drew the picture close to his eyes. He felt his dander rising as he recognized his granddaughter, his precious little Zorika, in the photograph. It was taken before her terrible accident, and she was pictured sitting on the lap of a certain violinist concertmaster of the Local Symphony Orchestra, named Ferdinand Lombardini.

And Ferdinand was not giving any lessons on how to play the violin. In fact, his renowned prized 1860 Vuillaume violin was sitting on a table, untuned and unused, in the unfocused background of the photo. In the foreground, all too focused for the viewer to see, were the knobby knees of Mr. Lombardini. And the reason these knobby knees were visible to the camera lens was because this despicable virtuoso violinist was not donning a stitch of clothing.

Mr. Olive's choler intensified to murderous levels as he discerned the evil intention of the photo. He didn't dare speculate what the accompanying VHS video would reveal. His eyes narrowed and his mind sharpened its focus to commit one single task. Hastily grabbing his walking stick, he got into his immaculately clean Mini Cooper, and did not wait for a genteel wave of a Port City resident to allow him to make a left turn out of the parking lot. Instead, he forced the oncoming drivers to slam on their brakes as he sped off to the Local Medical University with only one thought on his mind. He was going to kill that abominable, good-for-nothing scoundrel picaroon, Ferdinand Lombardini, with his bare hands.

CHAPTER 19

Any patients who were accommodated at the Intensive Care Unit of the Local Medical University and needing immediate and urgent attention would have to wait, for the medical staff was currently overwhelmed with the incoming injured tourists from the capsized boat that had met the fury of oncoming Hurricane Camille. The quickly expiring symphony violinist continued to lie in a coma, but now without the aid of his oxygen supply, and with his lone remaining kidney filtering less and less toxins out of his blood.

Without the amplified sound of his inhalations and exhalations, the room was relatively quiet with only a few monitors active, and the atmosphere was subdued, as Nonna had turned out the overhead lights before she left. This would be the last peaceful moment that Ferdinand would enjoy, even in his unconscious state, because the fuse over this powder keg was beginning to sputter.

The door to Mr. Lombardini's quarters was ajar, and the light from the nurse's station provided a backdrop to a lurking, ominous silhouette that registered a distinctive dark profile onto the floor that stretched from the doorway toward the center of the room.

This was a foreboding situation for the once well-loved and respected virtuoso musician, for as it turned out, the unhinged, vengeful and determined Mr. Olive with his myrtle wood walking stick, was casting the same identical shadow.

Only moments later, the unsuspecting Dr. Gamble was cheerfully approaching the doorway of the ICU with the black duffle bag filled with oxycodone in hand, whistling as he walked past the nurses' station.

"Hello, Nurse Shelly! I hear your bladder infection is healing, and your urine isn't bloody anymore. That's great news!" He bellowed as he strolled by.

He was expecting to meet Nonna in her son's room, to discreetly concoct a gentleman's agreement for the distribution of the illicit pills. This had put him in a sunny mood as he fantasized about traveling to the Swiss Alps with his dear wife for some invigorating cross-country skiing with the profits from the said entente.

As the Local Transgender Surgeon looked in the room of his comatose friend, he gasped as he saw Ferdinand twitching and contorting from grand mal seizures, and there was an alarming dark brown fluid filling the musical patient's catheter bag. Dr. Gamble's eyes widened further as he saw the condition of Ferdinand's swollen face, all the symptoms indicating advanced renal failure. He surmised, being a betting man that he was, that the chances of this patient surviving longer than ten minutes were very dicey indeed. He plonked the black duffle bag on the floor and reached for the button of the monitor to call out code blue over the sound system.

Unaware of Mr. Olive's presence in the ICU quarters, Dr. Gamble hadn't noticed that his poker game partner was in the corner of the room, searching for an extra pillow to use as a weapon to smother Ferdinand. Mr. Olive, in turn, was unaware that the duffle bag on the floor was nothing short of a pretty little item of confusion, since he had no way of knowing that the bag was filled with Mr. Eli Goldsmith's illicit oxycodone pills.

In his excited condition, Mr. Olive assumed that the guilt-ridden bag was filled with the nasty videos that he had just left behind at the storage shed. He concluded that the large, loud and embarrassing doctor had been a part of the evil activities against children, in particular, his own family member. And being not a man to forget a fancied slight, or to lose an opportunity of resenting it, he lunged at the Local Transgender Surgeon with the pillow, seemingly oblivious to the fact that the doctor was twice his size.

"Good Lord, Nazoon, have you lost your mind?" cried Dr. Gamble.

"Over my dead body will I let you get your filthy hands on those!" roared Mr. Olive as he pushed the pillow into the doctor's face, and kicked the black duffle bag, making it careen under the bed.

Dr. Gamble easily brushed the pint-sized Greek man aside with one arm. "Why, no need to be greedy, Nazoon. Calm yourself, I'm happy to bring you in on the profits of our venture. In fact, I believe The Constitution would even allow us to use these items to make our Monday night poker games more interesting!" offered the still jolly transgender surgeon.

"Why, you good-for-nothing bastard, that's my granddaughter on those tapes!" shrieked Grandfather Ya Ya.

"What on earth are you talking about?" cried out Dr. Gamble.

The Local Transgender Surgeon had no time to decipher his Monday Night gambling comrade's accusations or motives, for the two men were quickly closing in on combat. Mr. Olive grabbed a pen from his shirt pocket and began to stab forcefully and randomly at the doctor, which resulted in the Greek man taking a solid blow to the face that made a fearful impact.

The two began lurching around the room as their animus obscured reason and justice, knocking over equipment, and destroying everything in sight. Soon, the two men landed directly on top of Ferdinand, as the transgender surgeon tried to seize a long needle and wrest it away from the restaurant owner's hand.

The scuffle ended in a crackling climax as the bed's metal frame collapsed, and Ferdinand rolled out from under the two skirmishing men. With no handrail to stay his plunge, the comatose patient, in a befitting manner lacking of dignity, belly-flopped face down onto the floor with an impressive and fatal thud.

Chapter 20

Mahogany was deep in thought as he left the firemen's memorial service and decided to join Brother Ed who was eating at his usual spot at Table 13 in the Local Greek Deli. He was eager to share with the holy man his fresh perceptions of the world that made everything he looked at seem so iridescent ever since the dream he had the night of the fire.

Brother Ed was a Trappist Monk who lived at the Local Monastery established on a donated Southern plantation thirty miles north of town. He had reached the age of 75, and according to the rules of his diocese of the Roman Catholic church, he no longer had to follow a strict vegetarian diet. Once a monk reached these advanced years of life, Brother Ed learned, then he was allowed to eat meat. And eat meat he did. He ordered chicken gyro topping for his salad, a souvlaki with pork and lamb, and a steak kebab skewer on the side, every Friday like clockwork.

Brother Ed, being the most senior monk at the Local Abbey, had been recruited by the Mayor of Port City to oversee installing a formal, public memorial site in honor of the nine fallen firemen onto the beautiful, lush gardens of the monastery where he resided.

As Mahogany joined the friar at Table 13, he asked something that he had been wondering about. "Brother Ed, do you believe that God can be seen?" he inquired with a genuine sincerity that so moved the pious elder that he contemplated the question through the entire skewer of steak kebab before responding.

He wiped his white moustache and beard with his napkin, and replied, "Absolutely, Son. Without a shred of doubt, I believe that God can be seen."

Mahogany broke into a big grin and began to share his dream and its effect.

As the theological colloquy continued, it could be seen that The Fifth was pleased as punch with himself and his speech at the memorial service. Several devoted readers of *The Herald* were accompanying him out of the Tillman Auditorium to join him for lunch at the Local Greek Deli. His stride was that of a cat with a canary in its mouth, and he enjoyed gloating to his fans as they slapped him on the back, and quoted their favorite bigoted and supremacist slurs that they remembered from his improvised oration. The Fifth sat at Table 14 with his devotees, beckoned Laquita with a snap of his fingers, and asked her, "Say, Servant, where is Mr. Olive?"

His daughter looked at him, and for a moment considered punching his lights out, before finally responding with a sigh, "Ernest told me that our boss went to get some chicken from the storage shed, but that he became upset when he looked through a black duffle bag. He took off in his car. No one knows where he went or when he'll be back."

Nervous that Nazoon had discovered his secret, the Local City Councilman immediately abandoned his zealous admirers, and headed to the storage shed. He heaved a sigh of relief as he opened the wooden door and saw that his large black canvas bag was still where he had left it behind the top-loading freezer. As he was about to turn around, and go back into the restaurant, he spotted the black duffle bag full of videos thrown on the floor.

"What are these?" wondered The Fifth as he picked up the bag and began rummaging through it. Why, these are nothing but old videos. They don't even make the machines to play this VHS format anymore."

Just then he noticed the photograph of Mr. Olive's granddaughter, Zorika, pictured sitting innocently in a pink dress on top of the lap of the Local Symphony violinist who, it could not be ignored, was in the altogether, buck-naked.

Then he saw the label printed on the vinyl video cover: "Zora: Lesson 6," and it became clear to the Local City Councilman what nasty contents these VHS tapes must certainly occasion. Rather than being repulsed, his mind began scheming, as he saw the potential value of the videos being sold on the dark web as far exceeding the value of the secret he had already stored behind the top-loading freezer.

Suddenly, a wave of slick hucksterism was activated in his being, and as he took a few swigs from his flask, he hoisted the black canvas duffle bag full of VHS videos onto the bed of his American-made Dodge Ram truck, and began to carefully survey the labels on the vinyl covers with a cold, profiteering eye.

CHAPTER 21

Eli Goldsmith felt compelled to inspect his merchandise one last time before he evacuated from Port City ahead of Hurricane Camille. He descended the steps of the storm shelter next to the Old City Jail and continued down into the naturally formed underground edifice that harbored his connivance and thuggery. He was satisfied that even if the cavern flooded, nothing of importance would be lost. He then headed through the tunnel toward the trap door to the storage shed of the Local Greek Deli.

Even though States Rights Gist V was equipped with an ear so sharp that it never missed the softest vibrations of political gossip, somehow he failed to hear the Jewish cantor approaching through the tunnel underneath the trap door of the mountain granite storage shed. As the Local City Councilman tallied the potential earnings of the unexpected treasure he happened upon, he was quite unaware of any sinister maneuvers in his rear. Even when Old Heller began to bark ferociously at the sight of the holy man crawling through the trap door and approaching the truck, when he turned around, he did not suspect Eli of anything villainous. Just like the rest of the populace of Port City, South Carolina, States Rights was fooled by the Jewish cantor's studiously respectful front.

"Hey, what do you think you're doing, you thief! That's my property! Did you think that you could get away with stealing my merchandise?" demanded Mr. Goldsmith.

"Your merchandise? You? You are in on this with Ferdinand Lombardini?" asked The Fifth incredulously.

"Ferdinand? He thinks he can steal my merchandise, too? That good-for-nothing lazy pothead. He wouldn't know good product if it came and played his violin," snorted Eli.

"A lazy pothead with a penchant for children, I see. And you call yourself a holy man when you are cashing in on that?" replied The Fifth.

"What are you talking about, old man, have you lost your mind?"

And, so, a commencement of hostilities ensued.

While this pot came to a boil, Laquita overheard Mahogany describing his spiritual experience to Brother Ed, and came closer to Table 13 to listen in.

"I feel different now! I feel as if I've been given a magical pair of glasses that lets me see God's hand in everything," Mahogany elaborated as Brother Ed listened with an understanding twinkle in his eye.

Upon seeing Laquita, the viola professor at the Local Community College suddenly remembered the last part of the dream which he had totally forgotten.

"Laquita!" Mahogany exclaimed. "MarvLee was in my dream. He said something very strange. He said to me, 'Destroy the bag in the storage shed. Do it for Conner.' I wonder what that means?"

Laquita somehow was not surprised by this, and she had

an inkling what it could mean. She figured that from heaven MarvLee could see what she had already figured out about that black canvas bag in the storage shed with the sticky hair. She had puzzled over what it could be and concluded that it was a life-size sex doll, and that the sticky stuff she got on her hand was hairspray. She inferred that Mr. Olive, being a widower for so long, probably needed some relief. That's why MarvLee said to destroy that bag. She knew that her late ex-husband, the devoted father of her darling boy Conner, wanted to protect his son from ever seeing that disgusting thing by mistake.

CHAPTER 22

Back in the parking lot, The Fifth was sounding off like a man with a belly full, and the quarrel with Eli was assuming furious proportions. The councilman was increasing his salty language with spates of virulence and insults.

"I'm warning you, States Rights!" advised Eli. "You better keep a more civil tongue, or you are going to regret it."

But The Fifth could not resist an unkind thrust, and retorted with relish, "Who are you to talk of civility, you dirty Jew! You use little children, even Mr. Olive's granddaughter, you Hebe Shiksa!"

"Okay, that does it!" responded Eli at the ethnic slur that was beyond the pale.

He removed his yarmulke and carefully stuffed it in his pocket, snapping back, "So, States Rights, I guess you didn't know that I have a black belt in karate, did you?" After which fur began to fly between them.

Old Heller went berserk, yelping and growling, clawing desperately at the window to get out from inside the cab of the American-made Dodge Ram truck to attack Mr. Eli.

Ernest saw the commotion through the kitchen window, and the strapping Pacific Islander, who was normally calm and serene, who whistled with abandon in the kitchen, donning big smiles, abruptly transformed his demeanor.

Unknown to Mahogany, King, Laquita, Vladimir, or Mr. Olive, Ernest had come from a background of misanthropes and brutes. His family members were hardly models of rectitude, having all been trained in the saloon cut-throat arena of hoodlums that lived in the gang-dominated beaches of Micronesia, dealing in everything from illegal drugs to weapons. While The Fifth and Eli quarreled, Ernest's Micronesian relatives, all of unauthenticated DNA match, began arriving at the parking lot of the Local Greek Deli where they had been told to meet for evacuating the city.

The clan, with shaved heads, garbed in wife-beater t-shirts, exposing tattoos of various pack affiliations, chewing and spitting their native tree bark that was not legal anywhere in the lower, contiguous 48 states, did not exactly bring to mind for the onlooker the makings of a family gathering. They rather resembled an assemblage of toughs who, to the misfortune of Eli and The Fifth, were always itching for a fight.

Malik, who was skillfully trimming fat off a leg of lamb at the prep table, was watching Ernest leave the kitchen, and became suspicious at the change in his comportment. He followed Ernest and stopped at the back door of the Local Greek Deli to see the unusual activity in the parking lot, continuing despite the rain from Hurricane Camille increasing in volume.

As King stood there watching, stroking his lamb-trimming knife, he assessed the situation. He decided to text his thirteen siblings and sixteen uncles who all lived four blocks away.

"Come and watch. The Fifth is a' gettin' it!" He pushed the

send icon on his phone.

The entire brood appeared instantaneously at the chance to witness the racist politician, the bane of their existence, finally a'gettin' it.

Mr. Olive pulled up to his parking spot in the back lot, causing the Micronesian toughs to disperse around him. He was already in a bitter mood about his bruised eye, and still spoiling for a fight. For even though he came to understand that the black canvas duffle bag that Dr. Gamble brought to the hospital only contained some piffling pills inside of it, he still wanted to kill the producer of the nasty videos that featured his granddaughter.

He saw the Jew and the Southerner in a brawl by the storage shed and asked the Micronesians what was going on.

"They are fighting over who gets to sell the kiddie porn on the dark web."

No further prompting was necessary. Mr. Olive joined the melee with full gusto.

This was the moment that Laquita had been waiting for. Jane Margaret Gist grabbed the Nikon camera that never left her side since she arrived in Port City in the event that she could blackmail her father with compromising footage. As she pointed the lens and microphone at the parking lot tussle, and recorded accusations of kiddie porn, theft, and general illegal backstabbing, at last, she had proof that listed chapter and verse to what had previously been no more than innuendo. Her eyes became alive with enterprise as she continued to film the throng of struggling, cursing men.

She let out a little gasp when Eli went back into the storage shed and grabbed the Anschutz 1781 rifle. But then he looked at the sky, and could not distinguish through the clouds of the Hurricane whether the sun had set or not, in which case, he would not know for sure if he were violating the 39 rules of Mechalot if he fired the rifle, so he put it back down.

This is when Eli noticed the large black canvas bag behind the top-loading freezer, and deduced that this was what The Fifth was really interested in. With his adrenalized strength, Eli pulled the large, bulky bag out of the shed into the pouring rain.

"No! Don't bring that out! No one needs to see that!" shouted Laquita.

CHAPTER 23

Wondering where their fearless leader had disappeared to, the rabid readers of *The Herald* got up from Table 14 and went looking for the Local City Councilor. To their alarm, they discovered that their hero, The Fifth, was in the back parking lot surrounded by dozens of illegal immigrants, being watched by even more black folk, receiving karate chops from a Jewish man, and dodging punches from a Persian Greek man that they couldn't decide if he qualified as a white person or not. These wild-eyed rabble rousers, who already possessed undisciplined impulses that no one could curb, immediately donned their red "Make America White Again" caps, began frothing at the mouth, and joined the fight to defend their luminary. It quickly devolved into a free-for-all, featuring brass knuckles and knives, fists flying, bottles swinging, and the niceties of debate lost in a welter of howls and sulfuric curses.

By this time, Mahogany, Brother Ed, and otherwise fine-spun ladies and gentlemen of Port City who were happening by were drawn to the ruckus out back. Brother Ed, who could never satisfy his exacting sense of duty, attempted to calm down the rowdies with high-minded talk of compassion and forgiveness, which went over like a lead balloon. Just then, Mahogany recognized his stolen Double-bass being dragged out of the storage shed by Eli.

"Hey, that's my Double-bass! Did you steal that? Don't bring it into the rain; it can't get wet. That instrument is worth over seventy thousand dollars!"

As Mahogany grabbed his Double-bass out of the hands of the cantor, he lamented that the horse tail-hair on the bass bow had been pulled off of the stick, and was dangling out of the black canvas case. He hoisted the bulky and awkward instrument over one shoulder as he had done hundreds of times and ran inside of the Deli to keep the expensive instrument dry.

The Fifth yelled out after him, "I'm sorry, young lad. I had to borrow your bass fiddle for a spell. I had to sell it under the spur of a driving necessity. I would have eventually returned it to you once my gambling debts had been settled..."

The appearance of FBI Agent Jones on the scene at that precise moment caused a winding down of aggressions in the parking lot, possibly because the federal operative was pointing his handgun directly at Old Heller in the Dodge Ram truck. Even the toughest rascal from Micronesia could not conceal his soft spot for an innocent dog, and immediately released his grip off of the throat of Mr. Olive.

Old Heller himself recognized the moment as a good time to stop barking. He whimpered softly as he sat himself back in the cab and turned around several times while licking his lips nervously as he settled back onto The Fifth's pinstriped jacket.

Jane Margaret Gist recognized a grand opportunity had presented itself in Agent Jones. "Mr. FBI Man, take this camera and point it right there and keep filming. I want you and everyone here to witness this!" She then pronounced, "Councilman Gist, do you know who I am?"

As The Fifth was about to answer, she stopped him and

continued, "I will tell you who I am. I am your daughter."

A huge gasp of disbelief spread through the crowd.

"Yes, I am your daughter. And I know that you are aware that you have a daughter. Do you know how I know that?"

Jane Margaret reached into her bra where she kept a laminated document. It was a contract between her mother and States Rights signed shortly after Jane Margaret's birth. It was a contract that offered hush money. Latonya was to keep quiet about their daughter for a paltry price, so that no one would know that States Rights Gist had been on companionable terms with his black house servant. Jane Margaret knew when she wheedled this document from her mother that she could make use of the fishy aroma of this transaction that had lingered even after a quarter of a century. And she took great pleasure in seeing how it was having satisfying destructive results.

"So... DAD......I have been waiting for this moment for a long time. I am going to slap your cracker face!"

Jane Margaret then clobbered him on the nose with all her might.

At the sight of this, King and his thirteen siblings and sixteen uncles began to chant demands that the FBI man arrest him. The Fifth, seeing distraction as his only recourse for the moment, demanded that Eli Goldsmith be arrested for illicit pill sales. Mr. Olive then demanded that the FBI agent arrest whomever was responsible for those nasty videos of his granddaughter. Then Ernest demanded that The Fifth be arrested for stealing Mahogany's Double-bass.

CHAPTER 24

Mr. FBI man was not persuaded by any of these requests, for he bore strange tidings. As the Micronesian family, King's relatives, the knuckle draggers, and the finespun onlookers were becoming drenched in the downpouring of Hurricane Camille, he proclaimed the strange bodings.

"Ladies and gentlemen, these are sad days of demagogues, traitors, fanatics, idiots, and rascals in high places," he said with superlative understatement.

Agent Jones then turned to face The Fifth, and stated solemnly, "States Rights Gist V, you are under arrest for theft, arson, and nine counts of involuntary manslaughter."

Everyone gasped.

"The chemical lab determined that the Shack of Sit fire originated from the green metal dumpster behind the main showroom. Furthermore, they confirmed that the accelerant that started the blaze was a cake of bass-violin rosin. This tree rosin is used to make the hair sticky on the Double-bass bow in order to produce vibrations when the bow is pulled over the musical strings."

Mr. FBI man explained to the onlookers that when The Fifth stole Mahogany's Double-bass, he cleaned out the belongings in the case pockets. He took the cakes of rosin that Mahogany kept in the front pocket and tossed them into the dumpster behind the Shack of Sit before hiding the instrument in the storage shed. Then he set fire to the sheet music he found in the back pocket of the bass case and tossed that into the dumpster to conceal the traces of Mahogany's name. This small paper fire inadvertently set the highly combustible rosin on fire, which in turn set ablaze the even more highly combustible sofa parts that were in the bottom of the dumpster.

As Hurricane Camille began to pummel buckets of rain, everyone stood motionless, completely shocked that The Fifth was responsible, even if by accident, for the furniture store fire, and the deaths of the nine fallen firemen, one of whom was the father of his own grandson. By now, everyone had conceived an earnest loathing for States Rights Gist.

A painful skid downward in public opinion was occurring, and the Local City Councilman saw the writing on the wall that he was destined for a universal quarantine, even from his most fanatical groupies. This was a thrust to the heart rendered all the more lacerating because it touched his pride where it was tenderest.

While this explanation was happening, no one noticed that the Anschutz 1781 rifle was being positioned through the Local Greek Deli storage shed's door hinge, past the lurking green gecko, and aimed directly toward Mr. Olive. Just as the trigger was being pulled by the hidden figure, Ernest caught sight of the danger, and without a second thought, he threw himself onto Mr. Olive to protect him.

A hostile metal whistled dangerously close, but missed. The

trigger rapidly closed again by the unknown figure, and this time the next shot took effect, and Mr. Olive received a painful graze to his head as his Greek wool fisherman's cap took the brunt of the impact and flew into the nearby sago palm tree.

Mr. Olive was escorted back into the Deli by Brother Ed, who cleaned him up in the kitchen. In the parking lot, confusion and mayhem continued, Hurricane Camille made landfall, and lightning began to strike right as the shots were being fired. The mysterious shooter disappeared through the trap door of the storage shed.

Agent Jones was stalled as he put handcuffs onto The Fifth's wrists, and by the time he was done, everyone had scattered out of the parking lot of the Local Greek Deli, and left town on the evacuation routes with thousands of other residents.

For the next 24 hours, the town of Port City, South Carolina, was unsafe for man or beast. In the teeth of the wild winds and howling gales, the stress of the Category 4 storm drove to harbor along miles of shoreline, enormous tangled heaps of row boats, skiffs, dories, sailing vessels, launches, cruise ships, and mammoth container ships.

CHAPTER 25

A s with all hurricanes, the sun eventually came out again over Port City, South Carolina, and the birds began chirping their familiar songs. However, the fine-spun populace of the town would spend the next several months cleaning up the chaotic shambles left behind by Camille. Agent Jones had to drive to an upstate crime lab with the Anschutz 1781 rifle in his car, to be processed in order to reveal who had pulled the trigger, and thereby giving Mr. Olive the fright of his life.

"I need you to put a rush on this white substance lodged in the trigger, do you see it?" Agent Jones inquired.

"Yes. Very curious," replied the crime lab technician, who casually held it close to his nose and took a whiff, then removed a speck of it out of the gun and placed it on his tongue.

"I can tell you right now what this is," the lab technician revealed. "It appears to be homemade pan dulce."

About The Author

Fifth-generation Oregonian Dr. Charmaine Leclair, Ph. D. moved to Charleston, South Carolina, in 2002 to work as the orchestra librarian for the Charleston Symphony. Both amused and puzzled by the Southern culture of the Deep South, she noted the distinctive and humorous mannerisms of the Locals that contrasted with the transplants and tourists. She was inspired to put her observations together in this light-hearted satirical novel.

Leclair earned her Doctorate degree in Music History from the University of Oregon in 1995 and has been a cellist in the Hilton Head Island Orchestra (SC) since 2004. Charmaine lives with her husband, Ali, owner of a Greek restaurant, and their two cats at Johns Island, South Carolina.

NOTES

Beecher Stowe, Harriet. *Uncle Tom's Cabin*. Boston: John P. Jewett and Co. 1852

Menchaca, Ron and Glenn Smith. *Trapped: The story of nine Charleston firefighters' death*. Charleston, South Carolina: The Post and Courier. August 18, 2007.

Orden van, Kate. *Sexual Discourse in the Parisian Chanson: A Libidinous Aviary*. Journal of the American Musicological Society. (1995) 48 (1): 1-41.

Swanberg, William Andrew. *First Blood: The Story of Fort Sumter*. New York: Charles Scribner's Sons. 1957

Swanberg, William. *Sickles the Incredible: A Biography of Daniel Edgar Sickles*. New York: Ace Books. 1956.